A Baumgartner Reunion
By Selena Kitt

All rights reserved. No part of this book may be reproduced or transmitted in any form or by any means, electronic or mechanical, including photocopying, recording, or by any information storage and retrieval system, without permission in writing from the publisher.

This book is for sale to ADULT AUDIENCES ONLY. It contains substantial sexually explicit scenes and graphic language which may be considered offensive by some readers.

All sexually active characters in this work are 18 years of age or older.

This is a work of fiction. Names, characters, places and incidents are solely the product of the author's imagination and/or are used fictitiously, though reference may be made to actual historical events or existing locations. Any resemblance to actual persons, living or dead, business establishments, events or locales is entirely coincidental.

Cover Design: Selena Kitt
Cover Photo Credit: Jack Versloot
A Baumgartner Reunion © August 2009 Selena Kitt
eXcessica publishing
All rights reserved

Chapter One

"Sounds to me like you just want to have your cake and eat it, too." I listened for the sound of Beth waking up in the room next door as TJ cupped my mound over the sheet. The girl had some sort of extrasensory "Mommy and Daddy are having sex" antenna, and inevitably woke up for a glass of water or to go to the bathroom at the most inopportune times.

TJ's hand rocked the way he knew I loved, making me squirm. "Actually, I think it's eat your cake and have it, too." I rolled my eyes and snorted in the dark but shifted my hips toward him anyway. "Well, think about it. You can have your cake and eat it, but you can't eat your cake and still have it."

"All right, enough with the metaphor." I reached for his cock and found it already hard, and that made me smile—although I wasn't sure, suddenly, if it was the feel of my warming pussy under his hand that had effected him, or the conversation we'd been having about adding other people to our relationship. The latter made me suddenly want to cry.

TJ sighed, pulling the sheet aside. "Variety... it's the spice of life."

"Great, my marriage is now being reduced to a cliché." I slid my mouth down his belly, breathing warmth over the head of his cock and nibbling a little at the head, making him jump.

"I'm not talking about reducing it..." He groaned when my tongue slipped through the already wet slit at the tip. "I'm talking about expanding it."

"To include another woman?" I went back to nibbling, my teeth raking down his shaft.

"Other people, yes." His hand lost itself in the dark mass of my hair, pulling me back a little.

I sighed. "I don't want to see other people."

"Come on, Ronnie..." His hand massaged my scalp, his eyes tender but questioning. "We've been married for almost seven years. You can't tell me you've never been attracted to anyone else? I *know* you have!"

I blinked, trying not to think about the way Hector at work smiled and winked whenever I passed his classroom, how he often showed up in the tiny copy room the same time I did, brushing up against me from behind, his hand cupping the side of my hip, to get a ream of legal paper. So I felt a little twinge when he did, a warmth between my thighs, a tug in my belly. It didn't mean anything. It didn't mean—

"Just because I'm attracted to someone doesn't mean I'm going to act on it."

TJ's eyes searched mine, lazily rubbing the head of his cock back and forth against my lower lip. "But why not?"

"Because we made a commitment." I raked my teeth lightly across the spongy tip and he jumped.

"Don't be so literal." He rolled me over, pressing his weight onto me, opening my legs. I acquiesced with a sigh, loving the feel of his hardness rubbing up and down between my slit, but hating his words. "Our commitment is what we say it is…" His lips murmured against the pulse in my throat and I let my fingers brush the fine hairs at the back of his neck, soft as a baby. "I'm not talking about not loving you. I'm talking about sex."

His words were supposed to reassure me, but I felt my throat constrict. "So basically, you're saying I'm not enough for you."

"No, baby." He rocked, slow and easy—god, he knew how I loved that, opening me, a slow split, a gentle friction, up and up. "You're more than enough…"

More reassuring words—but why didn't I feel reassured? His mouth covered mine, the kiss deep and searching, his tongue slowly drawing me in, drawing me out, teasing me as he rubbed his stiff heat between my thighs. It throbbed there, insistent, making me squirm.

"God, you're so sweet…" His words were hot against my ear now, his teeth gently biting and tugging at the lobe.

"I never want you to think you're not enough, you're so very much more than enough..."

His cock found me with a shift of his hips, seeking entrance, and I gasped as he slid forward until he felt resistance, about halfway there. His breath caught and he gave a low moan that went through me like shiver, and still, he didn't stop talking, telling me... "There's no other woman like you. I want you and I want to share you, baby. I want the whole world to know how good you are, how sweet, how fucking hot..." He pulled back and plunged forward, so deep I clutched his shoulders, digging my nails in. TJ's eyes sought mine, dark and full of hunger. "How fucking *mine* you are."

It was true. It had been true from the first time we were face to face like this, much sooner than I had ever planned or anticipated—the rain had soaked us to the skin, but we hardly noticed as we peeled each other's clothes off and ended up on his living room futon instead of the big, soft bed upstairs in his room. It wasn't the tender or gentle or sweet thing I'd imagined—although he was all those things at turns—instead it was mostly heat and friction between us, a desperate need for more, always more with him. I could never get enough.

"Baby, look at me." I didn't want to, but I couldn't refuse him. I met his eyes, feeling the aching throb of his cock somewhere deep inside. "I'm just asking you to think about it."

I nodded, hating myself for doing it but unable to stop. I clutched him to me, wrapping my legs around his waist, my arms around his neck. My words were whispered, close to his ear. "Do you have someone in mind?"

He chuckled, moving now, his hips making easy circles. "Actually, no."

For some reason, those words *did* reassure me and something in me let go, gave in, my body melting against his. "So this isn't about wanting to have an affair?"

"I love you, Ronnie."

I felt that, in every movement, every moment, the way he slipped his arms under my shoulders, pulling me closer, wanting more. He did love me, he did want me—and I was so his.

"I want to get old with you and raise our daughter with you…and maybe fill that sweet belly with some more babies." His words thrilled me, and I didn't want to think about whether or not he knew it, or how much. My belly trembled against his, slick already with our sweat. "I'm not going anywhere."

Still, I wasn't ready to give in completely. "You just want to be able to sleep with other people."

"Come here." He rolled onto his back, taking me with him, sitting me up. His eyes swept over me and I felt satisfied at the dark look in them as they moved over my breasts, my waist, down to where we were joined, rocking. I couldn't stop—it felt too good—my hips making faster and faster circles. "I just want *us* to experiment…shake things up…" He groaned when I squeezed him with my muscles, spreading my legs wide to take him all, belly and balls deep.

"So you're bored?" I teased, leaning over him and arching my back, showing him my breasts but keeping my nipples just out of reach of his mouth.

"Veronica Mayer!" He didn't let me tease him long—that was another thing about him I loved so much. He didn't let me get away with anything. He shoved me off him, making me gasp when he pressed me to the bed on my belly, grabbing my hips and pulling me up to my hands and knees. I was too wet to resist him now and his cock slid in, punishing me with its length, making me gasp and clutch the sheet. "You're impossible!"

"No, I'm just selfish." I whispered into the pillow, lifting my hips to feel him in me, deeper, more. "I want this all to myself…"

I was sure he wouldn't hear me, but TJ chuckled. "Don't you teach your kindergarteners to share well with others?"

I didn't respond—I couldn't. I was beyond the point of talking or even wanting to think. I slid my fingers through my swollen lips, searching past the dark, wet fur toward my clit. TJ sensed my urgency, his hips moving faster—short, hard strokes that matched the insistent rubbing at my clit, his thighs slapping into mine. I moaned when he grabbed me and pulled me deep into the saddle of his hips, sinking himself as far as he could go.

"God, you know what I love!" He made me want to scream and I buried my face in the pillow, moaning low and loud, hoping Beth wouldn't hear us.

"That's right, baby," he murmured, moving my hand out of the way with his, strumming my clit with his big fingers, back and forth, round and round. "I know everything you like." He pinched my clit gently between his thumb and forefinger, peeling the hood of skin back and squeezing, just the right amount of pressure, like a pulse, over and over and over…

"Oh fuck!" I felt my orgasm hovering, teasing me, like a pregnant storm cloud waiting for just the right moment to let go with a torrent, a veritable flood. TJ didn't stop his tease, jerking my clit now as if it were a tiny little cock, his hips driving into me, pressing me forward on the bed. "Please, please, please!"

"Just imagine it, Ronnie…" He pressed me further, forcing my knees to buckle under his weight. "I could teach her to do all the things you love…"

I groaned into the pillow, shaking my head, trying not to imagine it but unable to stop the thoughts as his words flooded over me and his cock found some deep part of me, rubbing there again and again, as if my pussy were some magic lamp and he were searching for an elusive genie.

"Can't you feel her under you, baby?" Relentless, on and on. "Her tongue buried in your pussy, her cunt spread open for your mouth…"

The image was hot—more than hot, it made me burn with a deeper heat than I'd ever known with TJ alone. I wanted more, but I didn't want to say it. I didn't have to, though, because he didn't stop. He kept rubbing and talking and coaxing and crooning, telling me about her pussy and her tongue and her soft, hot body under mine, until I was aching for it, feeling it building low in my belly as I thrashed under him on the bed.

It had been years and years, but the memory came back like it was yesterday, the rich, lush feel of her body, the soft, smooth taste of her flesh. It was Mrs. Baumgartner I was imagining beneath me, with her smooth, tanned thighs, spreading them wide for my tongue. Oh my god, had we really—? I hadn't forgotten, not really, but I hadn't thought about it or spoken it of it since Gretchen and I had gone our separate ways.

"Oh Mrs. B," I whispered, lost in the fantasy, TJ's cock driving it home with every thrust. I could almost taste her, thick and pungent on my tongue, hear her moaning as I licked her to orgasm after orgasm after... "Oh god, yes, baby, that's my girl, come for me, come on, do it, do it, come in my mouth!"

TJ groaned at my words, his fingers digging deep into my hips. "Oh fuck, Ronnie, oh my god, yesss!"

I want to say it was the feel of him coming, that first, hot spurt of cum, that sent me over the edge—but it wasn't. It was remembering Mrs. B, the thick, hot lap of her tongue against my clit, and most of all, the feel and taste of her coming in my mouth, how she shuddered and dug her nails into my flesh and pressed her cunt against my face until I couldn't breathe, and I loved it, oh my god, I couldn't get enough of her...

"Oh, oh, yes, coming, oh please..." My voice turned small, young, and I lost myself in the memory and the sweet pulse of my orgasm, arching with it on the bed, again and again. Suddenly, I wasn't a twenty-nine year old kindergarten teacher, mother of a five-year-old, about to celebrate her seventh wedding anniversary—I was a young, naïve nineteen-year-old girl having her first experience with the wide open world of sexual pleasure.

I buried my face in pillow, panting and breathless, as TJ slipped out of me and slid off to the side. His belly was wet with sweat as he shifted his hips toward me.

"Wow." His lips found my hairline, my temple, my ear. "That was something else."

I didn't trust myself to answer, but I turned my face toward his. I was afraid of what he might see in my eyes, but I wanted the reassurance I was seeking in his. He gave it to me, too, nothing but love there as his fingers played through my hair.

I knew he was waiting for me to say something, so finally, I did. "I have to admit... thinking about it is kind of hot."

He grinned. "And if just *thinking* about it is hot, just imagine..."

I flushed, both with the thought and with the memory. I had never told TJ about what happened with the Baumgartners. Gretchen and I had been over for a year when I met him, and I had chalked it all up to some college experimentation thing. I wasn't a lesbian, I was sure of that. Yes, okay, I'd been attracted to women over the years, but—

"Ronnie?"

"Hm?" I turned onto my side and spooned up against him, pulling his arm across me, a protection, a barrier. I knew what he was going to ask, even before the words were out, and yet, somehow, they still surprised me.

"Who's Mrs. B?"

I froze, glad he couldn't see my face. *Well, Lucy, looks like you've got some 'splainin' to do.*

I cleared my throat, closed my eyes, my whole body on fire with the memories, and then I started to talk...

* * * *

'The headlights of my Intrepid reflected on the garage door and I turned them off, gathering up my purse and my bag with all my lesson plans. It was such a sweet moment of anticipation, the time between knowing I was home and going into the house where I knew TJ and Beth would be waiting. Knowing the long holiday stretched out ahead of us made it even better, and if it weren't for staying late to finish cleaning up the classroom and the fact I had a hamster in the backseat, it would be perfection.

I opened the side door and could smell TJ's spaghetti cooking. It just kept getting better and better! I swept in carrying the hamster cage, complete with hamster, and TJ stood up from the kitchen chair, his eyebrows raised as he moved instinctively to help. "Uh, what's this?"

I let him take the cage and he looked around for the best place to put it, deciding on the counter. He peered in at a little sleeping ball nearly the color of peach fuzz curled into one corner.

"Taffy, remember?" I began unslinging purses and bags from my shoulder, hanging them over a kitchen chair. "Classroom hamster. Jody Cornwell was supposed to take him home over Christmas break, but he has the chicken pox, and I couldn't get anyone else's parent's permission in time. Poor little guy had to wait in the car while I was visiting with Kathy after work—uh, and what's this?"

I stood staring at the glasses and the wine and looked up at him, pushing my hair out of my face and frowning. He uncorked the bottle and began to pour us each a glass.

"We're having a dinner guest." He offered me a glass of wine.

I smiled, my eyes questioning, and shook my head. "You know I don't like this stuff."

"Try it," he said, clinking his glass with mine.

"So do I have to guess who's coming to dinner?" I lifted the glass to my nose, wrinkling it at the smell.

TJ waited, watching me sip it, surprised as I took my first taste. "It's good, isn't it? I'll give you a hint. It's not Sidney Poitier."

"Then who is it?" I took another sip. "This isn't bad. Fruitier than most of the wine you've made me drink." I winked at him. "But it still tastes like alcohol."

I sat at the kitchen table, kicking off my heels. As often as I complained about them, I still wore them. TJ liked them, and I liked TJ imagining me standing in front of a classroom of kindergarteners in those heels. I looked up at him, waiting.

TJ took a gulp of his wine. "Gretchen."

"Who?" I set my glass on the table and stared at him. I knew. Of course I knew, after our conversation last week, what I'd told him about my week in Key West with the Baumgartners and the year that followed. Still, I acted surprised. I was surprised, really. How had he found her?

TJ began talking fast. "It wasn't hard at all, Ronnie. You could have kept in touch yourself if you wanted to. The Baumgartners still live in the same house, and Gretchen is still their nanny. Well, I imagine it's more like cook and housekeeper and stuff like that, now that the kids are teenagers. I just called the number in the phone book and asked for Gretchen. It was easy."

Easy. So the Baumgartners lived about twenty miles away from us, in the same house? I tried to imagine them, Doc and Mrs. B. And Janie and Henry, all grown up! My mind refused to wrap around the idea.

TJ took another gulp of wine. "Well, it's kind of funny how it all fell into place. Mrs. Baumgartner was thrilled to hear from me, and wanted to know all about how you were doing. Apparently, they're going on their annual trip to Key West over the holidays next week. I think that must be same the trip they took when—"

"You talked to Gretchen?" I stood, taking my glass to the sink.

TJ continued as if he hadn't heard me. "—when you went with them, the one you told me about? Yeah, I talked to Gretchen. She insisted on seeing you, wanted to call you, talk to you, but I thought... well, I thought it would be better to meet face to face."

I poured the rest of my wine down the sink, rinsing the glass and setting it on the counter next to the hamster cage. "You thought I'd chicken out and not meet her at all, didn't you?'"

"Maybe." He poured himself another glass of wine.

I turned to him, crossing my arms over my chest. "So you just decided to invite her to dinner without talking to me?"

"Honey, she practically invited herself," he replied, avoiding my eyes and taking another gulp from his glass. "There wasn't a lot I could do to stop it."

"TJ..." I sighed. "What did you think? She'd come over and we'd have a threesome on the kitchen table?"

"No." He laughed, standing up and putting his arms around my waist. "I just thought it would be nice for you to see an old friend."

I rested my head on his chest, putting my arms around him. "I just wish you'd... consulted me?" I lifted my head, suddenly aware of the quiet. "Where's Beth?"

TJ looked sheepish. "At your mother's."

I rolled my eyes. "Oh come on! I haven't seen a setup this obvious since Sidney Poitier showed up for dinner with Katherine Hepburn and Spencer Tracey."

"I don't think they had a threesome... did they?"

I pinched his waist, making him yelp and jump. "You know what I mean."

"I'm not up to anything. I swear it." TJ hugged me, kissing the top of my head. "I just thought you two would like to be able to talk about... well, whatever came up. Without having to worry about Miss Big Ears hanging around."

"Still, you didn't have to hide it from me," I said with a sniff. "It feels... icky."

"I—" I could tell he was about to deny it and he stopped. "I'm sorry. I can call her and cancel. I will if you want me to."

I raised my eyes to meet his. He was up to something, even if he was pretending he wasn't. Still, the thought of seeing Gretchen again made my skin tingle and my face feel warm. Did I want to cancel? The truth was, I wanted to see her again. The truth was, now that he'd opened the door, I wanted to see all of them again—Doc, Mrs. B, Janie, Henry. It was like some irresistible Pandora's Box.

"Let's just...take things slow," I said, my voice and eyes soft. "See what happens—" I pressed my cheek against his chest again, shaking my head.

"Okay," he agreed, hugging my shoulders.

"So, when is she coming?" I pulled away from him and went to retrieve my purse from the chair. "How much time do I have to get ready?"

"Only about half an hour," he admitted, looking at his watch. "She's supposed to be here by six."

"Well, then, I better hustle!" I flashed him a smile as I passed, heading for the stairs, already wondering what I was going to change into.

"Ronnie," he called, pouring himself another glass of wine. I stopped, watching as he poured another, too, leaving it on the table. "There's one more thing."

"What?" I asked as he lifted his glass to the hamster cage.

"Here's lookin' at you, Taffy," he said, drinking it and looking like he was wishing it was a shot of whiskey. Somehow I knew what he was going to say, although my breath caught anyway and my heart hammered at his words. "The Baumgartners have invited us to Key West with them over the holiday break." He tapped on the glass, trying to look nonchalant, and the hamster yawned, showing its long teeth before turning and snuggling back into the little nest it had made for itself in the cedar.

I didn't say a word. I couldn't. I just turned around and went upstairs, wondering just what I was going to do now.

Chapter Two

There wasn't any preparing myself, even if I told myself there was as I stood in front of the mirror and double-checked my hair and make-up, smoothed the brown silk skirt and tucked in my blouse. I was glad I was upstairs when she rang the doorbell. Just hearing her voice made my hands tremble and I pressed them to my thighs to keep them still as I paused at the top of the stairs.

"So nice to meet you!" Gretchen's smile was for TJ, but her look was just for me, and I knew it. She took a step toward the stairs, meeting my gaze with hungry eyes. I couldn't help my smile, even though it felt goofy on my face as I came the rest of the way down.

"Gretchen!" Her name felt familiar in my mouth, even after all this time. "You cut your hair!"

She laughed, snaking an arm around my neck and pressing her cheek to mine. "All of them—probably several hundred times since you last saw me, sweetie."

It was a very brief thing, that hug, but I could smell her hair, still white-blonde but cut into a short bob now, making her thin, pale face look fuller. She smelled fresh and sweet, like clover and oranges. How old was she now? I was doing the math in my head and came to the sum of thirty-four. Five years older than I was. There were the faintest lines around her eyes when she smiled, but she was still Gretchen.

"Come on in out of the cold." TJ shut the front door against the wind and snow, offering to take Gretchen's coat. Her dress was short, shimmering black in the lamp light as she shrugged her shoulders and let her coat slide off into TJ's hands. I knew she'd dressed for me, just like I'd dressed for her—and I think she knew it, too, the way her eyes moved over my blouse, unbuttoned into a suggestive V. She still had much more than I did in that department, the black fabric gathered between her breasts showing quite a bit of cleavage. I noticed TJ noticing as he poured wine and we sat around the kitchen table.

"Oh my god, Ronnie, you look so amazing." Gretchen smiled a thank you as TJ handed her a glass of wine. "I don't think you've changed at all."

"You haven't seen my stretch marks." I laughed, wrinkling my nose when TJ handed me a glass and setting it aside. "You look the same too—except all your hair is gone!"

"I got too old to get away with it anymore." She winked, taking a sip and turning appreciative eyes to TJ. "Mmm, this is good!"

"It's a petite syrah," TJ said with a nod.

Gretchen raised her eyebrows at him and lifted her little snub nose into the air in a delicate sniff. "And something smells *fantastic*." Her eyes were the same bright green, just as mischievous and not likely to miss a thing. Every time she looked my way, I felt it, like a familiar ache.

I took a long drink of wine and grimaced. "TJ's famous spaghetti—secret recipe, straight from his grandmother in Sicily."

"I'm so glad you called." Gretchen sat up and reached over to touch TJ's hand. It was brief, just a squeeze, but I noticed her long, manicured nails, painted bright red, an uncharacteristic color for her, and it reminded me sharply of Mrs. B. She turned her gaze to me again, and there it was, that feeling like someone had just reached their hand into my belly and twisted. "I've thought about you so often."

I held my empty glass out to TJ, who poured with a raised eyebrow. "I've thought about you, too." It wasn't a lie. When I'd first ended things with Gretchen, I thought about her all the time, and I knew it would drive me insane if it didn't stop, so I did what I needed to do. Vince, the guy I was dating at the time, was a personal trainer—gorgeous, ripped, he had a brilliantly rational mind but was more than a little OCD—and he taught me how to get rid of Gretchen for good. I'd put a rubber band around my wrist, and every time my thoughts turned to her, I snapped it—hard. Really, really hard. Sounds silly, but it worked. Between that and the incredibly huge eleven inch cock Vince presented me with to handle at every possible occasion—I've never had bigger, before or since—it was enough of a distraction to get me through. But the truth was, while it worked to keep me distracted, it didn't work all the time. No, not all the time.

Both of TJ's eyebrows were raised at me now and I tried to change the subject. "So, how are the Baumgartners? What's everyone up to?"

"Oh Ronnie, you wouldn't believe how big the kids are!" Gretchen smiled, shaking her head. I nodded, remembering them frozen in time: Janie as a gawky almost-twelve and Henry as a typical nine-year-old boy. Mrs. B had sent me a Christmas card that first year after Gretchen and I broke up, but then I moved, and the mail only got forwarded for so long. I still had that last photo tucked away in a box full of old diaries and journals marked: "Ronnie's Private: Keep Out." I remembered Janie's big front teeth and honey-colored ponytail, Henry's lopsided smile. Gretchen was still talking. "Janie's just gorgeous, she's got boys following her around like puppies. And Henry's huge, like his dad. You'll see—you're coming to Key West with us, aren't you? Carrie said she invited you…"

TJ and I both said "Probably," and "I don't know" simultaneously. Gretchen sipped her wine and looked between us, her eyes sharp.

I held my glass out for more wine. "I still can't think of her as Carrie. To me, she'll always be Mrs. B."

TJ poured me half a glass and then got up to check the sauce. I watched him stirring it, feeling warm and flushed and buzzed from way too much wine for me in too short a time. I noticed Gretchen watching him, too, and felt a twinge of something—jealousy?

"So how are Mr. and Mrs. B?" I asked Gretchen as TJ came to the table with a bowl full of spaghetti.

"Doc's practice is going gangbusters, as always." Gretchen held her plate out as TJ started to serve dinner. "With that bedside manner, though, go figure, right?" She winked at me and I smiled, remembering Doc's easygoing teasing, but mostly I remembered his eyes and the way they would follow me around a room wherever I went, as if he could see right through me. It suddenly occurred to me, as TJ sat down, that he and Doc shared a great deal in common when it came to looks and temperament. Funny how I'd never thought of it before.

"Carrie's real estate business hasn't done as well recently," Gretchen sighed. "The market is so bad right now. It's one of the reasons... well... things are changing for the Baumgartners. And me, too. Kids don't stay kids—can't be a nanny forever."

I nodded, feeling TJ's knees touch mine under the table as he sat and I gave him a smile. "Still, Gretch, you've been with them a long time."

"I couldn't turn down the money they offered, Ronnie." She shrugged, twirling noodles on her plate. "And, you know... all the fringe benefits."

That hung there, and I wondered if TJ understood as well as I did what she meant. It wasn't just the trips to Key West and Aspen and the New England Sound. There was so much more to working for Mr. and Mrs. B...

TJ cleared his throat, his eyes moving between us. "So why did you two break up?"

"TJ!" I nudged him under the table, my eyes wide.

"I'm curious..." He shrugged. "Are we not supposed to talk about it?"

"I don't mind." Gretchen smiled, but her eyes were pained, and I looked down at my plate, spearing a mushroom. "Ronnie found a boyfriend."

"The guy I dated before I met you," I explained, wondering if Vince even remembered my name anymore.

"You know how we girls have a tendency to abandon our girlfriends when a guy shows up," Gretchen teased. I wanted to say something, but the wine made my head feel fuzzy, as if it were too full.

"What about you, Gretchen?" TJ asked. "Did you find a girlfriend?"

"Or a boyfriend?" I chimed in, feeling desperate.

"Oh several." Gretchen winked at TJ but the look she gave me was full of a meaning I didn't understand. "Nothing lasting, though. I could afford to be picky, living with the Baumgartners."

I tried to imagine what it might have been like, if Gretchen and I had never broken up. Would she have stayed their nanny, then, I wondered? Would we all have been one big, happy family? The thought filled me with a mixture of longing, regret, and a deeper feeling I didn't even recognize at first—anger.

"This is the best spaghetti I've ever tasted." Gretchen's compliment made TJ blush and I smiled.

"He's a much better cook than I am."

"Like Doc?" Gretchen winked.

"Better." I touched my knee to TJ's under the table and he looked up at me, his eyes tender. "Although I admit, Doc could make a hell of a sandwich."

"Mmm god yes." Gretchen's tone changed and she gave a low, throaty moan that reminded me immediately what it was like between us. Her eyes met mine and they said it all. "He still can."

The double entendre didn't escape any of us. I couldn't help but remember—not only the night Doc and I snuck downstairs to make sandwiches and, while Mrs. B slept upstairs, he fucked me on the kitchen counter, but also there was the clear memory of being sandwiched between Doc and Mrs. B in more positions than I had ever imagined.

Gretchen's hand found my knee under the table and squeezed. She leaned forward, eager, earnest. "You are coming aren't you?"

I shrugged, not looking up. "I don't know, Gretch…"

"Oh, Ronnie, you have to come," she pleaded with both voice and eyes. "This is the last summer we're all going together. Henry's graduating this year, and I'm... well... things are changing. It would be so good, like old times."

I glanced at TJ. "I've never really left our daughter for so long..."

"She loves staying with your mother." He shrugged, no help at all. I knew what he wanted, what he hoped.

"You could always bring her...?" Gretchen suggested.

"No. Out of the question." I shook my head, adamant, and they both looked at me, surprised. I shrugged. "And really, I think two weeks is a long time to be gone..."

"I could stay here with her for a week," TJ offered. "Let you go out there for a week, and then fly out to meet you for the second..."

Gretchen brightened. "What a great idea."

"TJ..." I gave him a warning look but he ignored it.

"Something to think about..." He shrugged, filling my wine glass. I looked at it, already feeling way too buzzed to make any real decisions.

"You only live once," Gretchen prodded. Her hand moved over my knee under the table still, edging along the silk edge of my skirt. "We've all missed you, Ronnie."

I stood up, carrying my plate to the sink, murmuring. "Let me think about it."

I didn't want to think about it. I didn't want to think about anything. The wine had made me sleepy and way too relaxed, and when Gretchen curled up on the couch beside me and put her head in my lap just like she used to, I didn't say a word. TJ sat in the chair across from us, watching, listening to us talk—reminisce, really. It was as if someone had hit "pause" on the tape and had now pushed "play." We just picked up where we left off, soft voices. low laughs, inside jokes, our fingers twined together.

When Gretchen yawned, stretched and sat up, saying she had to get back, it was very late, and I didn't want her to go. TJ helped her on with her coat and her kiss goodbye was a little longer and too lingering to be called just friendly. She gave TJ a hug and thanked him again for calling. I knew it was coming and had planned my even, measured response to it, but when she said the words, mine wouldn't come.

"We're flying out Monday." She squeezed my hands in hers, swinging them, and it made me feel like a little girl. "Doc says just give him the word and he'll book your tickets."

"I—" They weren't there, those words I'd planned, the polite refusal, the kind turn-down. It wasn't just that I couldn't say them—it was as if they didn't exist anymore. "I'll let you know."

"Please." She leaned in and kissed my cheek, her lips brushing the corner of my mouth, making me shiver. "Please come."

With that, she was gone.

TJ closed the door, calling for her to be careful on the snowy stairs and then turned to me. "What do you think?"

I plopped down on the couch, still warm from where Gretchen and I had been cuddled together. "I think I'm in over my head."

"Time to grow gills?" He sat beside me and took my hand.

"TJ..." I sighed, not looking at him.

"It's sort of a once in a lifetime thing, isn't it?"

"Well, in my case, apparently...twice?"

He grinned, leaning in to kiss my cheek. "Lucky you."

"Yeah." I sighed. "Lucky me..."

* * * *

I knew I was really going to go through with it when I decided to shave everything down there. Honestly, I think I knew the moment I saw Gretchen again, but shaving was a symbolic act, a physical representation of a so-far ethereal decision. Doc had paid for our tickets, plans had been made, but it didn't feel real until I put a towel up on the bathroom counter that morning and handed TJ a razor.

"Everything?" He was used to trimming me, shaving the sides into a neat little landing strip, but I hadn't gone completely bare since that summer in Key West.

"Everything," I agreed, spreading my legs and leaning back against the mirror, hoping he wouldn't see the way my thighs were trembling or how wet I was already in anticipation.

The razor moved slowly, carefully, up one side and then the other, stripping me of a clear remnant of womanhood. It felt like turning back the clock in some ways, going back to that time when I was so young, so unknowing, so eager to learn. Still, there were things I couldn't un-know, experiences that had changed me forever. My body had changed, my hips fuller, my breasts, too, after nursing Beth for two years. I had stretch marks on my lower belly, now, soft plaits the remnant of my pregnancy. I knew there was no going back, even as I let him strip me bare in hopes that there somehow was.

"So smooth." TJ's fingers rubbed over my vulva, his eyes eating me up, hungry, and I wanted more than just his gaze. I would be on a plane in less than five hours—I'd insisted on a separate flight, wanting them all to have a chance to settle in for a day before I showed up—reunited with three people who, for that one glorious week that summer, had been my lovers, my teachers, my mentors. I couldn't even begin to imagine what might happen, but my body was strung tight, like a bow pulled taut, waiting to shoot some fated arrow.

"I'm going to miss you." I ran my fingers through his hair as he knelt and wiped me down with a washcloth, smoothing away any stray hairs. I could see my own clit when I looked down, my lips swollen and parted. It peeked up, as if asking to be touched, and the air felt cool and intrusive, a sensory overload.

"It's only a week." He kissed my thigh, his eyes still focused between my legs. Exposed, my pussy felt ornamental now, a showpiece, something I couldn't hide. It excited me.

"Anything can happen in a week." I gasped when his tongue flicked against my clit, quick, snake-like, a tease.

"Anything you want." He looked up at me, his big hands pressing my thighs open, keeping them there.

"Anything?" I raised my eyebrows at his carte blanche. We'd talked about it over the weekend, all the endless possibilities. I'd changed my mind a hundred times about going at all. We talked about setting ground rules, dismissed it and decided to play it by ear, only to come back to the idea of rules again. Everything felt uncertain, precarious, and it was both exciting and scary. We were on the verge anyway, with everything—his job was taking him to New York this summer, and I had just found a position in a private school out there. I didn't know what I was going to do with Beth. We didn't know anyone out there. I didn't know what I was going to do, and this vacation seemed like a push off a cliff I was already teetering over...

"I want you to have a good time." His breath moved against my pussy, warming me, making me tremble. "I want that most of all."

"Oh Teej..." It was my pet name for him, as if you could shorten his name or initials any more, yet I had found a way. I wanted to say something, to make everything good and right and perfect, but I didn't know the words, so I just pressed him to me, kissing his mouth with my pussy. He groaned, burying his face there, pushing my legs back, trying to get more.

"Oh god." I whispered the words, just letting him take what he wanted, what I wanted, what we both wanted—my pleasure. Still, after all this time, there was no one who could take me like TJ did, and I whimpered under his tongue, groaning as his fingers slid into me, seeking heat. There was no barrier to his mouth now, my lips parted for him, my clit seeming to tilt toward him. He flicked it, lapped at it, split me with both fingers and tongue, both of them meeting in the middle and then trading places, his fingers circling my clit, his tongue slipping down into my hole.

"Ahhhhhh god!" I cried as he began to fuck me with his tongue, his finger making quick work of my clit, back and forth, so fast it felt constant. There was no resisting him. My body knew what it wanted and he took it, shoving his tongue deep into my pussy as he made me come with his fingers rubbing my clit. The muscles in my cunt squeezed at him, sucking his tongue deeper, like a hungry, eager kiss as I came, my whole body shaking, my nipples hardening in surprise at the sudden sensation.

"Yeah, yeah, yeah," he murmured against my flesh, standing between my legs and rubbing his whole hand over my mound, making me let out a moan halfway between pleasure and pain. He was wearing boxers and his cock tented them nicely. There was a small wet spot around the head and I reached out to touch it with the tip of my finger.

"You want that, baby?"

I nodded, watching as he slid his shorts down, letting his cock spring free .It extended thickly against my thigh as he leaned in and kissed me. I could taste myself on his tongue and it reminded me of Gretchen and Mrs. B—the amazing, unmistakable, thick, pungent taste of pussy—and TJ seemed to know it.

"You like that?" He whispered the words as he slid his cock between my legs, nudging them further open. "The sweet taste of cunt in your mouth?"

I nodded against his shoulder, reaching down to grasp him, tugging hard. He gasped as I slipped the head of his cock up and down the now-smooth lips of my pussy, his eyes closing, his head going forward to my chest, clearly lost in the sensation. I tickled my clit with him for a moment before tilting my hips and sliding him into position.

"You like that sweet shaved little pussy?" I whispered as he shifted forward, sliding in. He groaned in response, arching, searching for more. I wrapped my legs around his waist, digging my heels into his behind and pulling him deeper. He shuddered, gripping my thighs and then shifting his hands up toward my pussy, sliding slowly out.

"God, that's beautiful." I could see him, too, thick and red, pulling back and back until just the head was inside of me. He massaged the smooth lips of my vulva with his thumbs, his eyes full of lust.

"Smooth as a baby," I murmured, wiggling against him. "Like some sweet young thing with the tightest little cunt you've ever been in." His eyes brightened at my words and I squeezed the head of his cock with my muscles, telling him I wanted more of him. He pressed forward, using his now-wet thumbs to rub my nipples, making me moan.

"God that's good." He rolled his hips into me again and again, watching his progress, in and out of my wetness. The sound of our bodies meeting, flesh against flesh, echoed against the wet tile and I leaned back on my elbows, fingering my own nipples as he fucked me, letting him do all the work. His thumbs eased my lips apart again, nudging my clit back and forth between them.

I looked up at his face, his eyes, the way he stared between my legs and my completely bald cunt.

"Would you like to see her fuck me like this?" I whispered, squeezing him between my thighs. He gasped, his eyes flying up to meet mine, and his reaction spurred me on. "See her strap on a dildo and get between my legs like this and fuck my bare little pussy?"

I knew he was imagining Gretchen—and god knows we'd played with enough toys between the two of us—but I had Mrs. B and her big black dildo in my head, her red nails digging into my thighs, raking over my hips. The image made me crazy with lust.

"She could fuck me while she sucked you off," I whispered urgently, squirming under him, getting into the fantasy. "Would you like that, baby?"

"Nnnnnnnngggg!" His fingers gripped my hips, just where I knew Mrs. B would hold onto me, guide me as she fucked me nice and hard with that thick dildo. TJ's words were just gone, his eyes and movements wild, driving hard into me, and I was getting lost, too.

"Fuck her mouth while she fucks my pussy, TJ!" I moaned, shoving my hips into his, closing my eyes. I could see her, all that honey-colored hair and those full, tanned breasts swaying as she fucked me, oh god, she was so beautiful on me, in me, all over me, I could smell her, taste her—I wanted her.

"Ohhhhhhh baby, I'm gonna—" I was coming, imagining TJ's cock was Mrs. B's dildo filling me, fucking me, taking me there as she slurped and sucked on him, making all those sweet Mrs. B noises that sounded like some little song, the sweet little blowjob hum she always did and I remembered so well.

"Ohhhhh fuckkkkk!" TJ grabbed me by the hair, making me gasp as he pulled me down onto the bathroom floor to my knees and shoving his cock between my lips. I knew he'd been imagining it, too—although I'm sure it was Gretchen's mouth and throat he was fucking, her big green eyes wide as she tried to swallow his length, her short blonde hair he was holding as he began to come, thick, hot jets of it over her waiting little tongue.

"Take it, take it, take it, take it," he whispered over and over, and I took it all, like a good girl, swallowing and swallowing, looking up at his face twisted in pleasure as he shuddered and panted against me. I didn't realize until later that I'd been making that same little humming noise in my throat that I remembered Mrs. B always did.

"Oh baby, come here," he murmured, gathering me up, sitting me on the counter again on the towel and pulling me close. My pussy felt juicy and swollen beneath me, exposed and vulnerable, and I remembered the feeling well from the very first time I'd shaved—when Mrs. B had shaved me and made me come that day with the shower massage, my body's betrayal.

He pushed my hair out of my face and kissed my cheeks, my lips, cupping my face in his hands. "I love you, Veronica. No matter what happens, I love you, and I'm never, ever going to leave you." I held onto him and felt it for the first time. It was not just reassuring, but real. I knew it was true, and it was enough. It would have to be.

Chapter Three

If I thought I'd been unprepared for seeing Gretchen again, nothing could have prepared me for walking back into the house I'd shared with the Baumgartners that week and seeing Mrs. B in her black bikini, smiling warmly and opening the door to my tentative knock.

I'd spent the whole flight remembering that week in December, as I watched the snow covered ground give way to clouds and then eventually descend into sand. Of course, they must have planned it. I knew that now, although I hadn't consciously realized it then. They asked me to come under the pretense of babysitting the kids, but that isn't really why I'd been invited along. It had been planned from the beginning.

How young I had been—how naïve. Mrs. B's slow seduction had worked like a charm—sunbathing topless and encouraging me to do so, too; letting me borrow one of her micro-bikinis and offering to shave me down there so nothing would show. How had they known I would slowly acquiesce the way I did, unable to resist her softness, both of them keeping me curious and on-edge about Doc until just the right moment when he finally came in between us, as if it were meant to be?

It wasn't until after it was all over, of course, that I felt manipulated. It wasn't until after Gretchen and I had parted, looking back on that week in Key West, when I realized I'd been used. The reality was Doc wanted a young, nineteen-year-old piece of ass, and his wife planned the seduction. So why, then, was I sitting on a plane, flying out to Key West once again, to stay with the Baumgartners?

The thought went through my mind as I stood in front of their door, waiting for someone to answer. The truth was, I didn't want to believe it was true. I wanted to think the Baumgartners really cared about me and what happened was as sweetly exciting and spontaneous as it felt—we were all swept away in the passion of it. Some part of me must have still believed that, because there I stood, knocking on the Baumgartners' door, and when Mrs. B answered, squealing and putting her arms around me, I leaned into her and sighed, and almost felt like crying.

"Oh Veronica, it's so good to see you!" Mrs. B kissed my cheek, her lips full and soft, catching the corner of my mouth as she turned her head. "Doc! She's here!" Mrs. B hadn't changed at all—the same honey-colored hair falling over her tanned shoulders, the same lush curves. I swallowed hard when she turned, holding my hand and leading me down the hall, seeing that her bikini was a thong, as usual, and she was completely exposed from behind.

"Look at you." Doc grinned as he came down the stairs, shaking his head. Doc was a little grayer around the temples, his dark curls a little less thick, but his smile was infectious, and his eyes swept over me, just like they always did, making me tingle. "Come here, girl!"

He swept me into his arms and squeezed, reminding me how big he was. I felt tiny in his arms, in spite of the ten extra pounds I'd put on since I had Beth. He kissed the top of my head and smiled down at me, his eyes sweeping over my outfit. I was dressed for a Michigan winter—long, gray wool skirt and a light pink sweater with soft brown suede boots.

"Did you bring your own bikini or are you going to have to borrow Carrie's?"

I smiled—I couldn't help it. "I've got my own suit, Doc."

"Well, then, let's see it!" He winked at his wife. "Everyone else is out swimming and we were just about to join them."

Everyone else. Doc pulled his shirt off and headed toward the door wall that opened up to the private beach in back. I couldn't help but notice his broad, tanned back, the thick muscles in his arms, and wondered how old he was now. My god, how old had he been back then? I heard Gretchen's voice the minute he pulled open the door.

- 30 -

"Janie, can I listen to your iPod?"

Everyone else included Janie and Henry, all grown up. I couldn't even imagine what they would look like. Would they even remember me? I was suddenly scared to find out.

"Come." Mrs. B took my hand and started leading me toward the stairs. "Let's get you settled in your room so you can change." I followed her up the stairs and down the hallway, a strange sense of deja-vu washing over me. The doors to what had been Janie and Henry's rooms when I stayed with them last were closed, but the three doors at the end of the hall were open, and I remembered those rooms very well—the bathroom, Mr. and Mrs. B's room, and what had been my room. Mrs. B stopped outside the junction of the three doors, as if we were at some crossroads, and glanced back at me.

"Gretchen normally sleeps here." She nodded at the room I had once occupied. "But she insisted on sleeping on the sofa bed downstairs so you could have this room."

"No." I shook my head, hefting my bag up over my shoulder. From this angle I could see into all three rooms—the huge Jacuzzi tub in the bathroom; the vanity with the tall mirror where I had watched Mr. and Mrs. B have sex; the bed I had slept in, often tossing and turning as I listened to the sounds of their lovemaking—and it really did feel like some sort of crossroads now. I had a decision to make, and it was suddenly clear to me. "I'm sorry, Mrs. B, but I can't do that. This is Gretchen's room. I'll sleep on the sofa."

She frowned, showing the lines around her eyes and her mouth more clearly than I remembered. "Are you sure?"

"Positive." Our eyes met and I saw disappointment in them. "I'll change in the bathroom and meet you out on the beach, okay?"

She nodded, turning and starting down the hall. I didn't watch her, but I was aware of her curves, the soft sway of her hips as she went down the stairs. In the bathroom, I made sure to lock the door behind me before I began to undress. I was Michigan-winter pale, but I didn't have any ambitions of getting a tan this time. Now I was old enough to concern myself about things like skin cancer and wrinkles and instead of lathering myself with baby oil, I slathered SPF 15 all over my nude body before pulling my suit out of the bag.

In spite of what I'd said to Doc, I didn't wear a bikini anymore. My suit had a low back and the front was an X that tied up around my neck, but it was a rather sedate brown one-piece that thankfully covered any hint of my stretch marks. I pulled my long, dark hair back into a ponytail with a Scrunchie and took a long look at myself in the mirror. The woman standing in the mirror was ten years older and wiser than the young girl who had once stood here in Mrs. B's borrowed orange bikini.

"Here goes nothing," I said to no one at all, shoving my discarded clothes back into my bag and carrying it downstairs. I left it at the end of the sofa along with my purse, like an announcement. I stood at the door wall for a moment, knowing the sun glinting off the glass would shield me from their sight, allowing me to watch unnoticed until I could get up my nerve to go out there.

Gretchen, wearing headphones and sunglasses, was stretched out on her back on a big beach blanket. Mrs. B had undone the straps to her bikini top and stretched out on her stomach beside her. I saw Doc wading out into the surf in the distance, and there was a young couple laughing and splashing each other down at the other end of the beach. I shivered in the air conditioning, pressing my hand to the glass, warm to the touch, wondering if I was ever going to gather enough nerve to open the door.

I wondered where Janie and Henry were when the young couple stopped their play and began running down the beach toward Doc. The woman was blonde, her hair almost the color of Gretchen's, but with a little more warmth, like honey. The way she moved, her hips swaying, her body's gentle curves, reminded me so much of—

"Janie!" I whispered, pressing my forehead to the glass. And behind her, of course, was Henry, tall and dark and broad like his father, with those same disarming curls. *It can't be*—even as my mind denied it, I knew it was them—even before Janie threw her arms around her father's neck and he swung her around, tossing her into the waves. I could hear her squeal, even through the glass. Both Doc and Henry laughed as she came up sputtering and wet, eyes blazing at her father.

"Daddy!" It was her voice, still, but different, older. Both Gretchen and Mrs. B looked up as I opened the door and stepped out onto the hot sand. "I didn't want to go in yet!"

"Too late!" Henry grabbed his sister by the waist and wrestled her back into the surf as she howled in protest.

"There you are!" Gretchen stood and held a hand out as I advanced. I took it, letting her kiss me, but turning at the last moment, so that her lips landed on my cheek instead of my mouth. She raised her eyebrows and then glanced down at my suit. She was wearing a black thong and matching bikini top, very like Mrs. B's. "Ugh, what's with the granny suit? How are you going to get a tan?"

I shrugged. "It's serviceable."

Mrs. B shaded her eyes, looking up at us. "You look pretty, Veronica." Her words sounded hollow to me, though, and she closed her eyes again.

"Come on, let's go in." Gretchen led me over the hot sand toward Doc and the kids. *The kids—ha.* Except they weren't such kids anymore. Henry was almost nineteen, and Janie had to be drinking age now, although just barely.

"Guess who's here!?" Gretchen's announcement was full of excitement, and I waited as they turned toward us, sure for a moment that neither of them would recognize me, or remember.

"Ronnie!" Henry exclaimed, his grin very like his father's. I smiled back at him, relieved.

- 33 -

When I turned to meet Janie's eyes, her mouth smiled, but her eyes didn't. She gave a little nod and just said, "Hi." It had to have been at least ninety out there on the beach, but I suddenly felt cold. Gretchen squeezed my hand and I looked at her, puzzled, but there was no time for any communication.

"Hop on babysitter!" Henry announced, lunging for me. I squealed and ran, going purely on instinct and habit, and just barely escaping the hand that grazed my arm. Unfortunately, he was taller and stronger than I was now, and caught up with me easily, wrestling me to the sand and pinning me under his big body.

"Good Lord, what have they been feeding you?" I gasped, barely able to breathe, but I was laughing, and so was he. The game was over much quicker than I anticipated as he rolled off me, sitting up and hanging his arms over his knees as he smiled down at me. I saw Gretchen, back on the blanket with Mrs. B, and Janie and Doc in the water.

"How ya been?" Henry asked, nudging me with his toe. "How come you never called us or wrote or came to see us or anything?"

Breathless, I half sat, looking over at where Janie was wading further out into the water away from us. Because of Henry's characteristic bluntness, which he clearly hadn't grown out of, it dawned on me why Janie's reception had been less than enthusiastic. I felt a twinge of guilt, biting my lip as I watched her dive beneath the waves.

"I..." My words felt caught in my throat and when I looked over at him and saw the confusion and hurt on his face, my heart lurched in my chest. "Oh Henry, I'm so sorry. I meant to, but... well, my life has been kind of... complicated... and very busy... since you were little..."

"Yeah?" He picked up a stick and started drawing circles in the sand. It reminded me of when they *were* little and we spent hours making sand castles.

"I guess you're not so little anymore." I knew I was stating the obvious.

"Mom said you got married and had a kid?"

I nodded, thinking of TJ and Beth for the first time since the plane had landed and I'd called to let them know I was safe. "She's five now."

"I guess kids make your life pretty complicated?" It was half question, half statement, and I didn't know how to tell him the truth, how to even begin.

I just shrugged. "Sometimes..." We were quiet for a while, watching Doc and Janie swimming, listening to the sound of the waves. All the time I'd stayed away, it had never occurred to me what they would think, how they would feel... I'd been too concerned with how slighted I felt.

"I'm glad you're here." The pressure of Henry's hand on mine surprised me. His hand was big, his fingers long, like his father's.

I smiled back at him. "I am, too." Even as I said it, I knew it was true.

"Last one in's a rotten egg!" Henry was racing toward the water before I could even take another breath and I swore softly, stumbling to stand in the sand.

"No fair!" I called after him, but he was already halfway to the water's edge, laughing over his shoulder at me.

The water was so much warmer than I expected and I groaned as I rolled to my back and floated in the waves. If nothing else, it was nice to float along with nothing else to do. It had been years since TJ and I had gone away somewhere together—since before Beth was born—and we never could have afforded something like this, a private beach on Key West.

"I miss that orange bikini..."

I opened my eyes to see Doc swimming toward me. I quickly stood, the water coming to my navel here.

"I'm too old to wear a bikini." I smoothed my hair back.

He gave a little laugh. "With a body like yours, sweetheart, you'll never be too old to wear a bikini."

The way he looked at me brought back the memory and the feeling of that week so long ago. I felt a slow heat spreading through my middle. Part of me wanted to be insulted by his comment, but another part of me was both flattered and excited by it.

"I guess I'm more self-conscious now than I was…then."

He raised his eyebrows, his eyes dark and knowing. "Well, we'll have to fix that then, won't we?"

"Hey, let's play a game!" Henry called over to us from where he was periodically splashing his sister just to annoy her. Janie had retrieved one of the floats and was sunbathing on it.

"I'm not *it!*" I called immediately, out of habit.

"Me, either!" Doc chimed in, winking at me.

Janie lifted her head, shading her eyes and looking toward me and her father. "I don't feel like playing." She rolled off the float and started wading toward shore, dragging it behind her.

Henry frowned as he watched her go, swimming over to us. "Maybe mom and Gretchen want to play?"

I sighed, watching Janie open the door wall and go into the house. "Maybe tomorrow, Henry." My eyes met Doc's and I looked quickly away. I didn't like the look in them, the questions or the knowing. "I think I'm going to go take a shower—wash off the jetlag and the salt water."

I didn't look at either of them as I began to wade toward shore, although I felt their eyes on me and was glad that my suit was so unrevealing. Gretchen lifted her sunglasses as I passed them and Mrs. B shaded her eyes.

"Where are you going?" Gretchen asked, propping herself up on her elbows.

"Shower." I opened the door wall, glancing back at them. "I'm tired."

I stopped at the top of the stairs, hearing music coming from Janie's room. I thought about going in and talking to her, explaining…but what would I say? I knew I would have to address it at some point this week, probably soon, but I felt suddenly exhausted and overwhelmed. I took a towel out of the linen closet and went into the bathroom. I intended to take a shower, but the big tub looked so inviting that I started to run the water in it, peeling off my wet suit and tossing it into the sink.

When the water was high enough, I turned on the jets and slid in, groaning as the water churned around me. I *was* tired, although less from the plane trip than from the anxiety and tension of the past few days. It had felt as if I were holding my breath, waiting for the moment when I saw the Baumgartners again, and now I felt deflated, like an empty balloon.

I floated in the warm water, closing my eyes and trying to block out my thoughts. But I was alone with them, and they were insistent. I couldn't help but wonder what might happen this week—or next, when TJ finally arrived. Mr. and Mrs. B's lifestyle clearly hadn't changed, and Gretchen… I remembered the way she looked at me, the comment she had made about Doc still "making a great sandwich." I knew all I had to do was ask—not even ask—just hinting or suggesting an interest would be enough to get the ball rolling.

I remembered the excitement in TJ's eyes when I talked about a threesome and I knew he wanted it. Maybe… I sighed, rolling my head around the back of the tub. I knew TJ loved me. I knew he wasn't going anywhere—he'd said so. What was I so afraid of? Opportunities like this one didn't present themselves every day. Maybe, I reasoned, we should just take advantage of it this once. Part of me believed that it might be enough to just… get it out of his system. Then we could go back to the way we were.

But could we?

The idea of opening my marriage scared the hell out of me, although I didn't want to admit it. Being part of a threesome, the way things had happened with Mr. and Mrs.

B... it was different. I was young and single. I'd had nothing to lose then. Who was it going to hurt? But now...

I sat up in the tub, eyes wide. What about Mrs. B? Was she ever jealous? Did she worry that Doc was going to fall in love with the nineteen-year-old babysitter and leave her? The thought startled me, and had honestly never occurred to me. How had she reconciled it in their marriage? I wondered if I'd been the first girl they'd ever seduced. How many others had there been? They were obviously still together, and they still cared about each other.

Confused, I leaned back in the tub, closing my eyes again. I couldn't imagine how I would feel, seeing TJ with another woman. But how had Mrs. B felt, seeing me with her husband?

I jumped when a knock sounded at the door. "Veronica?" It was Mrs. B, her voice concerned. "Can I come in?"

I glanced down, seeing the water churning around my breasts, my rosy nipples floating in the water, and smiled to myself. It wasn't as if she hadn't seen it before.

"Sure," I called.

She was still wearing her bikini, her body slick with oil as she came in and leaned against the sink. "Are you okay?"

I shrugged and nodded. "Sure, I'm fine."

Frowning, she cocked her head, her brow knitted. "Are you sure?"

I nodded again, not looking into her eyes. "Yeah. Just tired from the plane ride, I guess."

Mrs. B shook her head, coming over to the tub. She threw a towel down on the floor and knelt, leaning against the edge. I still didn't look at her, but I felt her eyes on me, searching. She rested her chin on her folded arms with a sigh.

"I don't think you're okay." Her voice was insistent and I swallowed when she touched my hair, smoothing it back from my face. "I think you are most definitely *not* okay."

I shook my head, denying it, a lump growing in my throat so I couldn't say the words.

"Hey..." Her voice was soft and kind, as it always had been, just like I'd remembered it. "It's me...you can talk to me..."

I shook my head again, blinking back tears. "No...Mrs. B... I..."

"Oh for Christ's sake, can't you finally call me Carrie?"

Startled, I looked up at her, meeting her eyes. They were teasing, but serious, too. I laughed, I couldn't help it, and she laughed with me.

"I mean, come on..." She smiled, cocking her head again. "We're both big girls, now, right?"

"Right." I laughed again, shaking my head. "Okay...Carrie..." Her name felt odd in my mouth, but somehow it was right. "I'm fine. Really."

We looked at each other and both burst out laughing at once, knowing it was the biggest lie in the world. And before I knew it, I was crying instead of laughing, tears streaming down my face, and Mrs. B—Carrie—was leaning into the tub to hug me.

"Oh sweetheart, it's okay," she murmured, stroking my hair. "Whatever it is, it's going to be okay."

"No it's not!" I sobbed, clinging. Her skin was slick with oil and my hands slipped on her shoulders, but I grabbed onto the strings of her suit. She did her best to comfort me, but I was crying hard, now, all the fear and emotion I'd kept inside for weeks pouring out over poor Mrs. B's shoulders.

"Yes, it will, I promise," she whispered, letting me pull her closer, so she was leaning half over the tub. "It'll be okay."

"You don't understand!" I croaked. "TJ wants to have an open marriage and I don't know what to do!"

She pulled back and looked at me, her eyes soft with understanding. Cupping my face in her hands, she kissed my tear-stained cheek, shaking her head. "Oh sweetie... yes... yes, I do understand."

"No!" I cried, feeling the desperation crawling up my throat with the words. "Carrie, I feel so caught! I'm scared to death of losing him if I do it and I'm scared to death of losing him if I don't—I don't know what to do!"

"I know." She nodded, sliding the rest of the way into the big tub, suit and all, and putting her arms around me. "Oh sweetie, trust me, I do know. I know just what you're feeling."

I curled myself against her, the water churning around us, and she rocked me, stroked me, cuddled me against her breasts and let me cry until my breath was hitching in my throat like Beth's did whenever she had a long tantrum and couldn't stop. When it finally ebbed, she pressed her mouth to my ear and whispered, "Ask me anything you want."

I looked at her, startled. It had occurred to me earlier that Mrs. B—god, I was going to have a hard time calling her "Carrie"—was perhaps the one person in the world who might really have a solution to my problem. But the first question out of my mouth wasn't about TJ or my marriage. It was something I'd wanted to know, something that had haunted me for years.

"Did you plan it?"

"Yes." She knew what I was asking, and she answered honestly. I sighed, feeling something in me shrinking. "But not in the way you think."

Puzzled, I looked at her.

"We loved you, Ronnie." Her fingers pushed my hair behind my ears, her eyes soft as they looked at me. "We still love you." Her words made tears come again and they fell silently into the bath water. "You were like part of our family, you'd been with us for so long. And yes, both of us... we were attracted to you. I'm not going to deny that."

"But inviting me here..."

"Yes." She nodded, touching my cheek. "We hoped...but if it hadn't happened...Ronnie, that would have been okay, too. We would have still kept loving you anyway." She smiled and then bit her lip. "Just... differently."

I didn't know if it was the truth, or if she was just saying what I wanted to hear, but it was important for me to know, especially because what I was about to ask her would affect me and my marriage for the rest of my life.

"Did you have it all planned out?" I asked, feeling a lump in my throat. "Did you talk about how... how you were going to..."

"No!" Her eyes widened, her mouth dropping open. "God, no! Of course not! We just... we just let nature take its course. And, thankfully... it did."

My feelings were a little assuaged. "Was I the first?"

"The first woman we were ever with, together?" she asked. I nodded. "No. We'd been to a few parties... we had a few... professionals. But you were the first... real person. The first one we'd ever cared for... aside from the physical."

"Really?" I blinked at her, surprised. I'd been sure, somehow, that I was just one in a long line of seduced babysitters along the way.

"And now we have Gretchen." She smiled, her eyes warm. "Who we also love very much."

I sighed, resting my head under her chin. "It's hard not to love Gretchen."

She chuckled. "True."

"Who wanted it first?"

After a moment, she said, "He did."

"What did you do when he told you?" I was remembering TJ telling me, my shock, my fear. "What did you say?"

"I was hurt," she admitted with a sigh. Her hand massaged my shoulder. "Confused... but the thought was exciting. We'd fantasized about it a lot, having another woman in our bed."

I nodded, swallowing hard. "We have, too."

"But you're afraid the fantasy is better than the reality?"

"Isn't it always?" I sighed.

"Was it with us?" I felt her lips brush the top of my head and smiled.

"No."

"I think it depends on the people involved." Her fingers moved through my hair, stroking, petting, and I felt my body melting against hers, finally relaxing. "I think it can be a big mess, or it can be an amazing experience."

"I don't want to clean up a mess."

She laughed. "I don't blame you."

"I'm scared," I admitted.

"I know." She kissed my temple. "It's okay to be scared. I'd worry if you weren't."

I shook my head, feeling tears stinging my eyes again as I choked out the words. "I love him so much."

"I know." She cupped my face in her hands, her eyes searching mine. "And that's what you need to trust."

"What do you mean?" I felt that desperation rising again.

"When it came right down to it, I had to trust that my love for Doc, and his love for me, was stronger than anything else." Her words were sweet, so sweet I could almost taste them.

"Was it?"

"Yes." She nodded. "It still is."

"Carrie..." I whispered her name and I knew my eyes were a question. Hers answered them, soft and bright and open.

Her voice was thick, like honey, like the color of her hair falling wet over her shoulders. "I like hearing you say my name..."

"Carrie..." I whispered again, leaning in to capture her mouth. She made a soft sound in her throat at the touch. "Carrie... Carrie... Carrie..." I whispered her name as I kissed my way down her throat, pressing myself between her thighs, feeling them open.

"Yes..." she whispered back, her hands moving down my sides, over my hips, pulling me between her legs. It was like coming home, and she welcomed me with open arms. I rubbed my face against the slickness of her breasts swelling over her bikini top. Her breasts were as bronze as the rest of her, and when I undid the straps and pulled them down, I found her dark-tipped nipples hard in spite of the warmth of the water.

"Oh god, Veronica," she moaned as I sucked one of them into my mouth. Her half-closed eyes watched my tongue trace a path around and around her areola, and she jumped and gasped whenever I flicked her nipple. Her breasts were incredibly full and lush and I used my hands to press them together, getting her nipples as close together as I could and licking back and forth between them.

Her hips bucked in response, her head going back and lolling on the edge of the tub as I worshipped her breasts. She was a goddess of flesh, and some part of me had always knelt at this altar, even in the years we'd been apart. My memories of her were nothing compared to the reality—wet, slick, luscious, moaning and arching against me, begging me for more. My whole body responded to her—not just my pussy, which was beginning to ache—as if it had come alive at her touch.

I hooked my fingers in the strings of her bikini, tugging them down the generous curve of her hips. She helped me, undoing the final strings on her top and tossing it aside, so we were both naked in the tub together. The feel of her body against mine was like slick velvet and my mouth sought hers as we slid together, limbs entwined, trying to get as close as we possibly could.

She tasted sweet, like oranges, liquid sunshine in my mouth as we kissed, our tongues playing together. Her thighs gripped my hips, strong and tight, pulling my pussy into hers, the heat of us together almost too much for me to bear. Panting, I broke the kiss, looking into her eyes. They were filled with lust, as deep and blue as the water we swam in, and I thought for a minute I was going to drown in them. There was no question what we wanted, what we were doing, and the excitement of the moment made my whole body hum with anticipation.

"I want you." Her words were soft but clear, her thighs tightening their grip. "I want you so much, Veronica... I haven't thought about anything else since you called."

"I know," I breathed, leaning in to kiss her again, tasting her sweetness. "Me, too."

Whatever darkness had been between us was gone, melted in the heat of our kiss. My body still felt so slight next to hers, all long limbs and arch, as if I could get lost in the plump softness of her flesh—and I tried, kissing her hard, pressing her to the far wall of the tub, rocking us in the heat of the swirling water. Her hands moved over my body, just accentuating our differences. My hips were fuller now than they had been then, my breasts, too, but they nowhere near matched her lush curves. My nipples were hard, pink, and pointed, and I moaned when she cupped my breasts, aiming them, rubbing our nipples together as we kissed.

"Oh, yes, Mrs.—" I stopped myself and felt her smile before she captured my mouth again, this time slipping a hand down between my thighs, cupping my mound.

"Oh sweetheart," she whispered, her finger probing between the smooth flesh of my lips. "You shaved..."

I smiled, searching between her thighs and finding her just as smooth, her lips fatter, fuller, filling my hand as I cupped her flesh. "Mmm, so did you."

She gasped when I slid a finger inside of her and moaned when I put in another, twisting them in her flesh. "Oh god, honey..."

"Stand up," I said, watching as the water slid off her body in sheets as she stood above me, her belly soft and tanned, her breasts heavy, her nipples hard. Water dripped between her thighs, down her legs, and I imagined it was her juices and longed to taste her. I knelt up in the tub, my hands kneading the curve of her hips, moving around to the swell of her ass.

Her clit liked to hide in the pink folds of her flesh, and I had to search it out with my tongue, making her squirm and moan. Her lips were swollen, completely smooth, and I kissed her pussy like a little mouth, sucking at her clit as if it were a tongue, flicking it, probing it. Her hands were in my hair at first, fisted in the wet length of it, pulling me to her, guiding me, but when she realized I wasn't going to stop, that my tongue was going to keep licking her, searching for her pleasure, she reached up to cup her own breasts, twisting and tugging at her nipples.

"Oh please," she whispered, her thighs trembling, her pussy clenching around my fingers. "Fuck me, baby, Finger my cunt!"

"You like that?" I murmured, sliding my fingers deeper inside of her, making her arch with pleasure.

"Yes, yes!" she panted, pushing her hips forward, wanting more. "Harder, oh, please, please!"

"Turn around," I said, using my hands to shift her, bend her over the edge of the tub. I spread her legs wider, looking at the smooth, swollen slit between them, the slightly creamy sign of her juices showing at the opening of her pussy. I put my fingers there, feeling her arch and press back onto them, sliding down past my knuckle, deep onto my hand as far as she could go.

"Ohhh yes," she moaned, fucking back on my hand. "Like that... fuck me, baby, yesss."

Still kneeling in the tub, I slid my tongue between her lips, slowly parting them, and then flattened it, using the tip to ease back and forth at the top of her crease while my fingers pumped in and out of her pussy.

"More!" she begged, her muscles tightening, releasing, squeezing my fingers. I slid another finger into her, feeling her shudder as she fucked back on me even harder, her breasts swaying beneath her, using her hands against the wall for more leverage. "Ohhhh god, fuck me hard, baby, hard, hard!"

I shoved my hand deeper, my tongue lapping between her legs, swallowing the wet sweetness of her cunt. She was making thick, guttural sounds with every thrust. I ran my other hand over the curve of her bronze, bucking ass, feeling the muscles there quivering with her effort. My pussy throbbed in response and I ached to touch it, but I slid my finger down the crack of her ass instead, finding the tight, puckered hole of her ass.

"Ohhhhhh fuck!" she whispered when I probed her there, making encouraging noises in my throat as I licked her, three of my fingers plunged deep into her pussy. Her asshole tightened around my finger, but her skin was wet and there wasn't enough resistance to keep me out. I slid my finger in to the first knuckle, feeling her whole body beginning to quake.

"Oh baby, baby, baby!" She moaned, moving her ass in circles now, rotating my fingers in her pussy, the one in her ass, and using my tongue against her clit to take herself there. "Yeah, that's it, baby, get me off! Ohhhhh god nowwww!'

I swallowed as much of her as I could, her pussy gripping my hand, her asshole a tight ring around my finger. I kept my tongue rolled over her clit, like a cup to catch her juices as she came, her hips bucking back, fucking me, her muscles squeezing every last bit of her come from her body.

She moaned softly and sank to her knees, panting, when I withdrew my fingers from her body. I smiled, sliding up behind her, putting my arms around her waist and resting my cheek against the damp honey of her hair. My nipples were hard against her back, my pussy throbbing, sopping wet now, after making her come, but I didn't care. I could have stopped right then and been satisfied, feeling her melt in my arms as she turned over, pulling me close to her.

"You always made me come so good," she murmured, brushing my hair out of my face and pulling my head to her breasts. She reached for the drain with her toes and pulled it, allowing the water to start to go down. I wasn't done with my bath, and knew she would want to wash the oil off her body, but I didn't say anything as we waited for the water to drain, the warmth giving way to chill everywhere my body wasn't touching hers.

When the water was just a few inches deep, she began to kiss me down onto my back in the big tub, her body soft between my thighs, her belly pressed against mine, our nipples touching as we kissed. Her tongue made hot trails over my neck and chest. I gasped when she found my nipple, sucking and licking first one and then the other.

"Touch yourself," she whispered as she settled herself between my thighs. "I want to watch you."

I bit my lip, but my pussy was on fire, aching to be touched, and I slid my hand down to part my lips, opening my slit and showing her pink. Her eyes were full of lust as I began to pet myself, rubbing the hood back and forth, easing the skin over the sensitive bud of my clit. I used just one finger, first back and forth, then around and around, moving faster as the sensation swelled.

"You like it so sweet," she murmured, kissing my thighs as she watched. She raised her head and cocked it, smiling down at me. "Do you want me to lick you?"

I whimpered, arching, and spread myself wide for her. "Please... yes, please..."

She lowered her whole mouth down into me, her tongue flat and sweeping over my pussy, up and down my slit at first, spreading my juices. I heard her swallowing them, making soft, hungry noises in her throat as she worked her way through my flesh. I moaned out loud when she found my clit, moving her tongue back and forth now through my lips.

"Ohhh yes!" I cried, my hand fisted in her hair. "Oh god, Carrie, yes!"

My body was wet, my nipples hard from the chill, but I didn't feel cold at all. In fact I felt flushed with heat, as if there were a furnace inside of me, something ignited deep in my belly. I looked down at her kneeling between my legs, her ass up in the air, her heavy breasts swaying as she fastened her mouth to my pussy and sucked. I thought I'd never seen anything so beautiful in my life, and I wanted her—I wanted more of her, all of her.

"Come here," I urged, holding my hands out for her, eager. She understood, easing her way up and then around, the tub more than big enough to accommodate us as she spread her legs over my head. I could smell her and the taste of her cum lingered still at the back of my throat as she pulled my legs back and buried her face between them again.

I knew I wouldn't be able to hold out long against the sweet, aching feel of her mouth, but I tried, concentrating on her pussy, spreading it wide with my fingers and teasing her clit with my tongue. Her clit was smaller—perhaps the only thing on her body less endowed than mine—and it liked to hide, especially right after she'd come once, or when she was very, very excited. I had to wrap my arms around her full hips and pull them into me, my mouth covering her pussy, my tongue probing deep between the soft, pink folds of her flesh. Her clit was tiny, a little bud of flesh hidden in the wetness, but I found it and I stayed fastened there, determined.

I knew I'd found the spot when she began to rock her hips, moaning against my pussy, her tongue losing its rhythm on my clit, giving me a little reprieve. I was dangling on the edge, so close to coming I felt as if I might burst, but I wanted her, too, I wanted to feel her come in my mouth, I wanted the sweet flood of her juices all over my face.

"Nnnn! Nnnn! Nnnn!" It was all she could say with her face buried between my legs, her tongue taking my clit past the edge now, the first quivering thrust driving my hips up against her mouth. I was coming, oh god, coming so hard I couldn't breathe, I couldn't think, my whole body bucking with sensation, like a hot, wet bubble bursting in my belly and flooding down between my thighs.

"Ohhhhh Carrie!" I moaned, lost in the feeling, forgetting all about her sweet, throbbing pussy, but she reminded me, using her own fingers to spread herself wide, making that same, "Nnn! Nnn! Nnn!" I fastened my mouth to her clit with a groan, licking her fast, the same lightning rhythm again and again, until she lost it, too, her mouth coming off of me as she whispered my name, followed by, "Come on, come on, come on," and then she was there, her whole body shuddering with the force of her orgasm. She thrashed and twisted on top of me as she came, rubbing her cheeks and face over my still-throbbing pussy, making me gasp. Finally, she was still, panting on top of me, her heavy breasts pressed into my belly, her cheek resting against my thigh.

"I missed you," I heard her whisper and I felt tears stinging my eyes.

I nodded, although I knew she couldn't see me. "I missed you, too." I felt it, in every part of me, how true it was.

She kissed me softly when she sat up, and then led me to the shower stall in the corner. We spent a slow, luxurious fifteen minutes soaping each other up and rinsing each other off.

She got out first, saying, "I've got to start dinner. We're having lasagna."

"Sounds heavenly!" I called through the steam, watching as she wrapped herself in a towel and went out of the bathroom.

I dried myself off, realizing then that I hadn't brought up any clothes—I just had my bathing suit to put back on. I opened the door, thinking to ask Mrs. B—Carrie, I smiled at the way I corrected myself, even in my head—to bring my bag upstairs. That's when I saw Janie standing at her door, her eyes fixed on me.

My heart lurched and I opened my mouth to say something, but all that came out was, "Oh. Hi."

Janie's eyes darkened as she glanced at her mother's bedroom door, and then back to me. I realized she must have seen her mother leave the bathroom and my chest tightened.

"Right." She blinked, and I wondered, for a moment, if she was blinking back tears. Then, she shut the door, and the radio went on—loud. Too loud.

"Fuck," I whispered, glancing at the Baumgartners' closed bedroom door, and then shutting the bathroom door. I leaned against it, feeling sick, closing my eyes. Janie's opinion of me was bad enough, I thought, without her seeing... what *had* she seen? I wondered. What had she *heard?*

"Ronnie!?" It was Gretchen's voice, calling up the stairs. I sighed, opening my eyes. I'd have Gretchen bring me up something to wear, I decided. And then... then... I looked at myself in the long, steamy mirror over the double sinks, not sure I even recognized myself.

Then, I decided, I'd figure out what to do next. Whatever that might be. I'd cross that bridge when I came to it.

Chapter Four

"I can't believe she's even old enough to have a boyfriend." I leaned in to whisper my words to Gretchen as we cuddled together on the couch. Gretchen's head was tucked under my chin as we shared both a spoon and a pint of Haagan-Daas—just like old times.

"Time didn't stop when you left, you know." Janie tossed the length of her honey-colored hair over her shoulder and gave me a long look before turning her attention back to both the movie and her boyfriend.

"Ouch," I winced, blinking back tears when Henry gave me a sad, sympathetic look from where he was stretched out on the floor near his sister. Of course I hadn't meant for Janie to overhear me, but it seemed as if the girl had superhuman powers when it came to listening, especially to anything I said.

"Teenage hormones," Gretchen whispered, spooning a big bite of cool chocolaty goodness into my mouth. "She can't help it."

"Shut up, Gretchen."

"Come over here and make me," Gretchen retorted, matching Janie's snotty tone.

"Hey, come on, it's a good part." Janie's boyfriend glanced at us, frowning. Brian was a good-looking kid, no doubt about it, tall and tanned and dark-haired. He reminded me of Doc in a lot of ways, especially the sharp, mischievous look in his eyes. He didn't miss much, that one, and I'd felt his eyes on me more than once during the course of the evening.

"Then pay attention to the movie instead of feeling up my sister," Henry snapped, nudging Janie from behind with his foot. She stuck her tongue out at him over her shoulder and snuggled closer to Brian. Something was going on under the blanket the two lovebirds were covered with, I was sure, but in the absence of the girl's parents—Mr. and

Mrs. B. had gone to bed early—I had been pointedly ignoring it.

"You still want me to make some popcorn?" Brian nuzzled Janie's neck, leaving feather light kisses there and over her chest. She was wearing a halter top that left the tops of her breasts exposed above the blanket.

"Please?" Janie smiled up at him, and I felt a tightness in her chest. It was the same look Janie used to give me as a little girl when she wanted something, the sweet puppy-dog eyes and slight pout. Except she wasn't such a little girl anymore, was she?

Brian leaned in to kiss her and I swallowed hard as I saw their tongues touch, Janie's body arching into his, her arms twining around his neck. The boy had to be hard as a rock, laying so close to Janie like that under the blankets—and who knew what was going on underneath them? The thought made me flush, and it wasn't from embarrassment, even if I tried to convince myself it was.

"Anything for you, baby," Brian murmured into Janie's hair.

"Not the microwave kind!" Janie insisted, wrinkling her nose at him as Brian got up. I couldn't help but see the bulge in his shorts, even though they were denim and enveloped him in quite nicely. "Real popcorn. With *real* butter."

"I can make it, if you want to stay and watch the movie," I offered to Brian from the couch.

"No, thank you." Janie's head snapped toward me and her eyes narrowed. "I don't want your popcorn."

"Real popcorn with real butter, coming up." Brian turned and headed toward the kitchen while Janie snuggled back under the covers, curling her arm around so she could rest her head on it.

"Here." Gretchen plied me with more ice cream and I attempted a smile as I took the creamy bite. "It's almost gone. We're such pigs."

"Oink," I agreed, watching as Henry lifted the edge of Janie's blanket and slid underneath it.

"What are you doing?" Janie sighed as Henry slipped an arm around her waist.

"I'm cold." Henry settled in behind her and Janie sighed again, but accepted him spooning her, snuggling her back against his chest and twining her fingers with his.

"You'll have to move when Brian comes back."

"I know." Henry shrugged, glancing toward the doorway where Brian had disappeared. I could hear the whir of the air popper. "You smell like coconut."

"My shampoo, I think," Janie murmured, her eyes on the screen where Tom Cruise was playing, of all things, a Nazi.

"It's nice," Henry breathed, dipping his face a little closer to Janie's head.

"Last bite," Gretchen said, scraping the spoon across the bottom of the ice cream carton. "Want it?"

I shook my head, frowning as I watched my former charges snuggling together on the living room floor. I had noted and tolerated Brian's advances—Janie was old enough, and he was her boyfriend, after all. But this? Henry and Janie were brother and sister, but they were lying together like... like... I glanced at Gretchen, who appeared unaffected by their closeness. Obviously this happened all the time. But for siblings, it seemed like they were too familiar, too...intimate. Much more than I was comfortable with.

"Quit being so mean to Ronnie." Henry's whispered words weren't meant for my ears, and I knew it, but I heard him anyway. Janie didn't answer him, her eyes on the television screen, but I saw the way her jaw tightened. "She loves you, ya know?"

"Funny way she has of showing it," Janie breathed, tossing the blanket aside as she stood.

"She's so impossible." Henry sighed as his sister stalked out of the room, joining her boyfriend in the kitchen.

"She hates me." I was surprised at how steady my voice was.

"She doesn't hate you," Gretchen countered, leaning over to put the ice cream container on the coffee table. "She's just mad. She'll get over it."

"Does anyone else want popcorn?" Brian poked his head through the doorway to inquire and I smiled at him.

"No, thanks."

"I do!" Gretchen waved her spoon at him. "Me! Me!"

"You're going to get fat." I laughed, pinching at Gretchen's nonexistent stomach.

"Gretchen can out-eat me *and* Brian put together," Henry scoffed, shaking his head. He stood and announced, "I'm gonna get a Coke," before heading toward the kitchen.

"I don't know where you put it." I watched Gretchen as she stretched, cat-like, her top pulling up out of her shorts to reveal a tanned expanse of belly.

"I have a hollow leg." Gretchen smiled as she slid back against the couch cushions, the blanket pulling down to reveal the length of her tanned legs.

I raised an eyebrow. "I don't remember that."

"What do you remember?" Gretchen cocked her knee and traced a line with her finger down her inner thigh toward the hem of her shorts.

"Quit," I hissed, glancing toward the kitchen. Gretchen wrinkled her nose at the warning and ignored it, using her finger to slide her shorts aside a little, revealing the fact that she wasn't wearing any panties. Her pussy lips were shaved smooth, and I glimpsed the familiar pink. "You're bad."

"I know." Gretchen moved back under the blanket, her hand sliding up my bare thigh, her words whispered close to my ear. "You make me wanna be really, really bad."

I groaned softly when Gretchen's fingers pressed the seam of my jean shorts, rubbing there.

"Popcorn!" Brian announced, coming back into the room with two full bowls. Gretchen eagerly reached out to take one and settled happily next to me, already munching.

Brian flopped on the floor beside Janie, who sat on the floor stirring popcorn around in the buttery bowl.

- 54 -

"Did we miss anything good?" Janie asked, licking butter off her fingers.

"It's a Tom Cruise movie," I snorted. "There couldn't have been anything good to miss."

Janie turned to look at me, making a face. "Don't be mean to my Tommy."

"Who are you now, Rosie O'Donnell?" Henry scoffed.

"Do I look like Rosie O'Donnell?" Janie glanced over her shoulder at him, her blonde hair a cascade down her bare back. She was still wearing the bikini she'd swam in earlier in the day and Henry's eyes swept over her, darkening.

"No, sweetie, far from it." I frowned when I saw Henry's very unbrotherly look. "Besides, I think Tom Cruise is too old for you."

"Ha. He married Katie Holmes, didn't he?" Janie tossed a kernel of popcorn into the air and caught it quite delicately on the pink tip of her outstretched tongue.

"She was a child bride," Henry grumbled, popping the top on his can of Coke and taking a long, loud sip.

"Well, I'm not a child," Janie countered, but she was looking not at her brother, but at me.

"I know," I murmured, but Janie had turned her attention back to the popcorn, the movie, and her boyfriend.

Brian hushed us with, "I can't hear the movie!" and I refrained from further comment about Tom Cruise's acting ability when Gretchen's fingers slipped under the edge of my cutoffs.

Being under the blanket made me feel entirely too warm, but I didn't dare throw it off, and Gretchen's teasing made me even hotter. I thought the end of a movie, Tom Cruise or otherwise, had never come soon enough.

* * * *

"Want to go up to my room?" Gretchen whispered as she slipped under the covers and spooned me from behind. I murmured something indefinitive in my sleep, snuggling back against her in spite of myself. The house was quiet and dark, and I didn't know how long I'd been sleeping on the pull-out sofa in the living room. Henry had fallen asleep before the movie's end, and when Janie and Brian decided to go out after it was over, Gretchen had woken him and sent him off to bed.

When it was just the two of us, Gretchen helped me pull out the couch bed, and we'd said goodnight. But when she bent her head to my ear to whisper, "I'll come down later," as Janie and Brian got ready to go—I didn't say no. I already knew what was going to happen. Whatever resistance I'd managed to hold onto had disappeared.

"What time is it?" I murmured, blinking in the darkness. Gretchen slid her hand up under my t-shirt, stroking the soft skin of my stomach.

"A little after two." Her lips found the sensitive spot behind my ear, the one she knew made me melt, and I did just that as her tongue made fat lazy circles there.

"We shouldn't be doing this," I whispered, tilting my head anyway, to give her better access. "Did Janie and Brian come back yet?"

"I don't know." Her hand moved up to cup my breast, and I gasped when she thumbed my nipple. "And I don't care. I can't wait any longer. I've been thinking about you all night."

"They don't let him stay overnight here, do they?" I asked, turning in Gretchen's arms, trying to distract her.

"No." She sighed, recognizing my tactic, but she grabbed my hip and pulled me toward her, twining her long legs with mine. "Not that Janie hasn't asked, but the Baumgartners wouldn't let him. His parents are staying at the Marriott"

"He seems like a nice kid." I tried to ignore the way her hand moved over my hip, stroking lightly, her finger edging at the elastic of my panties.

"He is."

I closed my eyes as she began to feather kisses over my cheeks, pressing my lips briefly with her soft ones before kissing a trail down my throat. I couldn't concentrate, although I kept trying. "Gretchen, can I ask you something?"

"Mmm?" She didn't really answer me as she licked the length of my collarbone, making me shiver.

"Do you think…have you ever wondered if something's going on between Janie and Henry? Something that…shouldn't be going on?" I voiced my concern hesitantly and waited.

"What kind of…" Gretchen's head came up and she frowned at me in the darkness and then laughed. "No! Of course not."

I swallowed and shrugged. "They seem…awfully close."

"They are close," Gretchen agreed, tugging at my shirt, leaving it pushed up that way just under my breasts as she shifted and began kissing my ribcage. "But, Ronnie, come on, they're brother and sister!"

"I know that, but…" I sighed softly as she made a fast circle around my navel with her tongue. "You know… Mr. and Mrs. B are so free… sexually, I mean… ohhh!" Her fingers had found my nipples beneath my shirt, rubbing back and forth over the material the way she knew I loved. I couldn't believe she'd remembered. "I just wondered if maybe…"

Gretchen squeezed both my nipples in her fingers. "I've never seen or heard anything."

I gasped and bit my lip as she nibbled her way along the edge of my panties. "What about tonight, the way they were laying together on the floor?"

"They do that all the time." Her fingers were rolling my nipples now, teasing, her breath hot on my mound as she settled herself between my thighs. "It's just the way they are."

"I guess…" I breathed, trying to remember my concern, trying to remember what or why I was even questioning things. "Maybe… oh Gretchen…" Oh god, her mouth, my body remembered her mouth like it was yesterday, and she wasn't playing anymore as she pressed her tongue against the wet crotch of my panties. "Oh god... oh... maybe... maybe...I'm just being a prude."

"I know." I could hear the smile in her voice. "We're going to have to fix that."

"You're doing a pretty good job."

"I can do better."

"I know you can."

The memories rushed in almost as quickly as my pussy flooded with juice as Gretchen nuzzled my panties aside and probed me with her quick, pink tongue. Everything was so familiar, the press of her hands spreading my thighs, the soft noises she made as she delved deeper into my flesh with her mouth. We'd spent the better part of a year as roommates and lovers and even if I'd tried to block it out—and I admit now, I had tried—it all came back in a warm, wet deluge as we writhed together on the little pull-out couch-bed.

"Lick me, too," she begged, shoving her panties down her hips and positioning herself above me. "Oh please, I want your tongue, I love your tongue on me." Her mouth was already buried in my pussy again, my panties gone now and my legs spread shamelessly wide, my hips rocking up against her tongue.

It was dark, but not dark enough that I couldn't see the wet spread of her smooth, shaved lips, the glistening heat of her flesh drawing me in, warming my cheek as she rolled her hips around and around. I explored her with my fingers first, rubbing the thick hood of flesh covering her clit, making her moan against my pussy.

Oh god, she was so good. She knew just what to do with her mouth, and I gasped when her fingers slid into my wetness, first one, then two, her tongue never leaving the sweet spot at the top of my cleft. Her scent was making me dizzy with lust, and I wondered if the soft spread of her thighs ended at the apex of heaven...or hell.

"Please, Ronnie," she moaned, spreading wider, lowering her pussy toward my mouth. "Oh, god, I've missed you so much, baby, please, please…"

Her pleading voice, her body so soft but insistent on mine, were more than enough to convince me. Still, I was tentative at first, licking through the wet folds of her flesh first, getting used to her taste, then savoring it. Her tongue lashed against my clit again and again, sending me to dizzying heights, toward a place I couldn't breathe, couldn't think, and didn't care.

"Oh yesss!" She shuddered with the first touch of my tongue to the sweet button of her clit and I began to lick her, slowly at first, moving the nub of flesh back and forth, then faster as she began to rock and moan. I could feel her breasts pressed against my belly, her nipples hard, and I squeezed my own, sending shockwaves down to my aching clit.

"Gretchen," I managed to whisper in the darkness, the flutter of her tongue about to send me over, and she knew the sound and feel of me about to come, she knew, because she quickly focused her efforts, her mouth covering my mound and sucking hard on my clit. "Ohhh fuck! Ohhhh!"

I remembered where we were and tried to be quiet, burying my face in the musky taste and smell of her pussy to muffle the sounds of my orgasm as I bucked underneath her. I shuddered with the sensation, my pussy throbbing, but she didn't let up, her mouth fastened tight, sucking every last bit of my climax from me.

"Stop, stop," I begged, pushing my hips up, trying to free myself, the feeling too much now. She turned quickly, not letting me transition from floating, distant pleasure to more immediate thoughts, straddling first my thigh, and then shifting so her pussy rubbed teasingly against my own still pulsing one.

"Remember this?" she whispered in the dark, and I broke, then, nodding, reaching for her. I couldn't deny it anymore. I remembered…everything. The taste, the smell, the feel, the sound of her, and there was nothing that could keep me from her now.

"I missed you so much," I confessed, pulling her close, kissing her deeply. She made a soft noise in her throat as our tongues touched, her hips moving in slow, distracting circles.

"I'm sorry," I gasped when we broke for air and she sat up on me again, rocking. "I was so stupid… just young and stupid…"

Gretchen pressed her fingers to my lips. "Shh. You're here now. It doesn't matter."

I didn't quite think that was the truth, but I didn't argue as she pulled my hands up to her breasts and rubbed her pussy against mine, back and forth, the wet, slapping sound of our flesh filling the room. Her nipples were hard and I rolled and pulled at them, making her rock faster between my legs.

"Make me come," she whispered, as if I were doing anything—she was doing all the work, riding faster, harder, her breath coming in shallow gasps. "Oh please, oh baby, now, now, now…"

I squeezed her nipples hard and she arched, quivering as her climax began, her pussy trapping the heat of it between us, her body bucking, giving it to me, as if she could force her orgasm into or through me somehow. I held her as she came, when she collapsed onto me, breathless and still trembling, her body covered with a fine sheen of sweat.

"Oh my god," she murmured, cuddling into me, pulling the covers up over us both. "I forgot…" She kissed my cheek, my chin. "So good…"

"Mmm," I agreed, closing my eyes and trying not to feel the wave of guilt that washed over me suddenly, trying not think about TJ, trying to remember that he'd given me permission to be doing just this, reconnecting in just this way with an old friend…and lover.

"I don't want to lose you again." Gretchen's voice was small and my eyes opened at the sound. I didn't know what to say to her. I had no idea where any of this was going...and maybe I didn't want to know. But I was filled with regret for hurting her so long ago, and wanted, somehow, to make it up to her.

"I'm sorry," I whispered, hugging her shoulder, pulling her close so I could kiss the top of her head. "I'm just so sorry."

The silence stretched and I stroked her hair, wondering what she was thinking. I didn't know how she couldn't hate me for finding some guy and taking off on her like she'd been some bad dream I didn't want to remember. I hated myself for it, I realized, glad for the darkness covering the red heat of my cheeks.

"I'm going back to school starting in January," she declared, sounding proud.

"You are?" I smiled. "What for?"

"Photography."

I nodded, smiling now, too, remember the amazing pictures she took. The Baumgartners Christmas card was always one of Gretchen's photos.

"Wow. Good for you, Gretchen."

She shrugged. "Can't be a nanny forever."

"I guess not," I agreed.

"I'll be in California for two years," she confessed, snuggling closer. "But I don't want to lose touch again, like we did..."

I sighed, shaking my head. "It was my fault..."

"I don't care," she insisted, kissing the top of my breast and sliding a leg over mine. "I just don't want to lose touch. Promise me."

"I promise," I whispered. "I'm so sorry."

"Stop." She lifted her head to look at me. I saw the glint of her eyes and wondered if she had tears in them, like I did. "I love you, Ronnie. I always have."

"Yeah," I choked, kissing her and feeling one of her tears—or was it mine?—slip between our lips. "I always loved you, too."

Satisfied, she snuggled back down under the covers, still holding me close. We stayed that way a while and I wondered if I should send her to her own bed, wondered what the Baumgartners would think if they woke to find us like this... But it was silly, of course, to worry. They'd known about me and Gretchen...they'd known all along, and encouraged it.

"Goodnight, baby," Gretchen whispered sleepily, and the soft sound of her deep breathing that followed decided me. I didn't care who saw us, who knew. So we'd been lovers, were lovers now, still. Where was the shame in it?

"Goodnight," I whispered back, although I knew she was already sleeping.

I must have drifted off, because the next thing I remembered was Janie standing next to the couch bed, the stairway light on, giving the room a half-lit glow.

"Janie?" I asked groggily, shading my eyes against the light, seeing she was still wearing the same clothes she'd had on when she left with Brian. "Are you just getting in?" I wondered what time it was.

"Well, you two look cozy," she snapped, curling her lip. "Goodnight."

"Janie!" I stage-whispered, trying not to wake Gretchen, but Janie was gone, stomping up the stairs and slamming her door, in spite of the late—or early—hour.

I spent a long time staring up at the ceiling in the darkness and wondering what to do about Janie. It wasn't until I had given up racking my brain for some sort of solution that I realized Janie's eyes had been red from crying as she stood there. But why? I didn't know. I didn't know anything anymore, except that it seemed like a long time until morning.

Chapter Five

"Hello?" I whispered, flipping my cell phone open and hanging half over the side of the couch bed. I'd found my ringing phone in my purse on the floor and managed to answer it just before it went to message.

"Hey baby, you awake?"

TJ. I smiled at his sleepy tone and knew he was still in bed. "I am now," I whispered, sliding the rest of the way off the couch bed, where Gretchen was still sleeping. The girl could sleep through anything. Of course, I'd finally been sleeping just as hard, having spent most of the night tossing and turning, thinking about Janie and Gretchen and the Baumgartners and just what in the world I was doing here in Key West in the first place.

"In your own bed?"

My stomach clenched, even hearing the teasing tone in his voice.

"Of course," I admonished, giving a guilty glance over my shoulder at Gretchen's sleeping face, my eyes traveling over the slope of back, down to where the sheet met the curve of her hip. Damn, she was sexy.

"Alone?"

I bit my lip, grabbing my shorts from their resting place under the couch bed and yanking them on, juggling the phone.

"Not answering that one, huh?" TJ chuckled as I stood and tiptoed to the door wall, opening it to reveal the early morning rise of the sun. It was a gorgeous morning, the breeze warm on my face as I shut the door behind me. The sky was streaked with fiery oranges and reds and I stood there for a moment, breathless at the sight.

"Come on, you can tell me," TJ urged, his voice lowering even more. "Did you spend the night with the Baumgartners?"

"You're hard as a rock just thinking about it, aren't you?" I teased, walking down two short steps and across the patio to sink my feet into the softness of the beach sand.

"You know I am." His voice was slightly hoarse. "I miss you."

"I miss you, too," I confessed, and I did. I could almost imagine myself in his arms, my fingers walking that sweet, dark line down his belly toward his cock. God, I missed that, too, the feel of him filling me. "I spent the night with Gretchen."

He actually gasped. "Really?"

"Yeah." I kicked at the sand as I began walking toward the water. "Really."

"...And?"

I smiled. "And it was...good."

"Good? Just good?" TJ snorted. "You can do better than that!"

"Well..." I bit my lip, bringing up the fresh memory of the night before, the soft feel of Gretchen's skin, the sweet, pungent taste of her pussy. I could still taste her in my throat. "She came down to my bed in the middle of the night..."

"Uh-huh."

"You really want to hear this?"

TJ groaned. "Hell yes! Tell me."

"Tell me first," I murmured, feeling the gentle throb of my pussy, already responding. I hadn't managed to find my panties and the seam of my shorts rode up between my pussy lips as I walked. "Are you hard?"

"Uh-huh," TJ murmured.

"Are you stroking it for me, baby?" I closed my eyes and pictured him, cock in hand. The thought made me dizzy with lust.

"God, yeah," he groaned. "I woke up hard for you, and now I can't stop thinking about you with Gretchen..."

I smiled, walking toward the water. "Thinking about us kissing..."

"Mmmm…"

"Undressing each other…" The waves were cool over my bare feet as I hit the water's edge.

"Mmm-hmmm…"

"She's got gorgeous breasts," I admitted, remembering the weight of them in my hands. "Firm…full…hard pink nipples…"

"Oh god…"

I could hear his breath coming faster. I imagined I could hear his hand shuttling up and down the length of his cock and ached to lick off the pre-cum I knew was accumulating at the tip.

"And they're very sensitive," I told him, his groan of pleasure spurring me on. "She loves to have them sucked—hard."

"You're killing me," he whispered. "God, I'm so fucking hard."

"Her pussy is totally shaved," I said, walking along the wet sand at the water's edge. "You'd love it. All wet and pink. Her little clit likes to hide, and she loves being licked."

"I bet she does." He growled softly into the phone and I knew, I just knew he was squeezing his cock hard in his hand, prolonging things. "Did you lick her good for me, baby?"

"She was on top of me at first," I confessed. "Licking my pussy…"

"Mmmm I miss your sweet little pussy." His words made me shiver. "Did you like it?"

"Oh god, yes…" I curved around a large expanse of tall rushes and shoregrass on my walk, letting the dew at the edges wet my outstretched fingers as I passed. "Her tongue is so good, TJ. I forgot how sweet it was to be with a woman."

"Better than me?"

I made a face he couldn't see. "Don't ask me that."

He chuckled. "Go on… did you return the favor?"

"I did." I smiled. "Her pussy tastes so good... I forgot how warm and wet and sweet..."

"Mmm... more..."

"She makes these little noises when she's about to come," I told him, glancing behind me toward the house. It was out of site now—I'd walked a ways down the beach and the vegetation obscured my view. I wondered if I was still on the Baumgartner's private beach at all. There was nothing but sand and vegetation behind me, and in front of me as well. The next house was barely visible in the distance. "She always asks me to make her come, almost every time, 'Make me come, Ronnie, make me come...'"

"Oh that's hot," he moaned. "Did you?"

"Not with my tongue."

"No?"

I grinned, anticipating his reaction. "She wanted to rub our pussies together."

"Oh my god." He growled into the phone, a deep, sudden sound, and I knew he was holding back his climax. "Are you touching yourself, baby? Rub your little clit for me..."

I glanced around, up and down the beach. Did I dare?

"Go on," he urged. "I'm so fucking hard for you. Tell me more."

I sat on the sand, away from the water line, close to the edge of the expanse of shoregrass, and unzipped and unsnapped my shorts. My pussy was aching to be touched.

"I love it when she rubs her pussy with mine," I murmured, laying back in the sand and sliding my hand down into the V of my shorts. "Her little clit kissing mine like that..."

"Mmmm...yeah... more..." TJ's breath came faster through the phone, in short, hard bursts.

"I watched her ride me like that," I went on, my fingers finding the already wet, aching bud of my clit and rubbing it. "Her breasts in my hands, her nipples so hard... her breath coming faster..."

"Faster..." He urged, groaning softly.

"Yes..." My fingers rubbed faster, my hips moving with the motion, as I remembered Gretchen's wetness against mine. "Her pussy rubbing there...soooo wet...soooo good...all that pink, hot flesh... again...and again..."

"Oh fuck, Ronnie!" TJ gasped and I knew he was close. Just the sound of his voice sent me straight to the edge and my nipples hardened and tingled under my t-shirt.

"That's how she came for me," I whispered, slipping my fingers deeper into my pussy. "Just like that."

"Ohhh god, yeah, make her come."

"Riding my pussy with hers, fucking me..." I fucked myself faster, deeper, harder, whispering my words to him as the waves crashed against the shore and the sun spread its light across the sky. "Giving me all her juices – I could feel them running down my thighs..."

"Oh baby! I'm coming! Ohhhh fuck!"

I made a soft noise in my throat as I listened to him, the growl of him making me shiver even in the dawning heat of the morning.

"Yes," I whispered, closing my eyes, seeing him pumping his cock in his fist, him cum spilling over in hot waves. What a waste, I thought with a groan. I wanted his cum, I wanted to play in it, lick him clean, swallow him whole. My orgasm was a sudden, sweet surprise, and I bucked my hips toward the sky as I came, not bothering to muffle my moans as my fingers probed deep into my flesh, my quivering pussy aching for the hot, full pulse of TJ's cock.

"God I love you," I murmured as I cupped the heat of my mound with my whole hand.

"I love you, too." I could hear the lazy, post-coital smile in his voice. "Did that really happen?"

"Yeah, pretty much." Of course, I hadn't told him that I'd also had a bathroom encounter with Mrs. B... "Are you jealous?"

"A little," he confessed. "But only because I couldn't be there to watch."

"Just watch?" I teased, zipping my shorts back up. My fingers were wet, and instead of wiping them off, I licked them clean, recalling the taste of Gretchen in my mouth.

He chuckled. "Well, I wouldn't say no to an invitation to join you."

"You're really okay with all of this?" I sat up and shook out my hair—full of sand.

"More than okay," he agreed.

"You're okay with me and Gretchen..." I mused, looking across the water at the rising sun. It was brighter now, truly almost morning. "What about me and... say... Mrs. B—er, Carrie?"

"Yep."

I bit my lip and pushed my luck. "Me and Doc?"

"Sure. Why not?" His response surprised me. We'd talked about a threesome with another woman... but he was okay if I slept with another man while he wasn't even around to supervise? "Sweetie, this is your freedom vacation. I told you that before you left. Anyone you want, you can have."

"*Our* freedom vacation," I reminded him, standing and brushing the sand from my shorts. "You're still coming aren't you?"

"Yep, my bag's already packed."

"How's Beth?" I asked, debating which way to walk. I was probably off the Baumgartner's beach, but I continued on anyway, not quite wanting to go back and face everyone in the house quite yet.

"She's good. She misses you."

"I miss her, too."

"But she's looking forward to a week at grandma's." There was a short pause and then he laughed. "Speak of the devil, I hear her now. I better go before she tries to get her own Frosted Flakes again."

I smiled, remembering how much trouble little Miss Independent could get herself into in a very short amount of time. "I'll let you go. Call me later?"

"Count on it. Love you, babe."

"Love you more." I smiled.

"I love you more, too," he said, saying what he always said when I told him I loved him more. "Bye."

He'd hung up before he could hear my goodbye, although I said it.

I slipped my cell phone into my pocket and was about to turn back to walk toward the house when something caught my attention out of the corner of my eye. There were three old cabanas spaced evenly on the sand on the other side of the cover of the tall rushes and shoregrass. The vegetation was almost thick and tall enough to hide me completely, even if I was standing, and it might have been tall enough to hide Henry, too, if he hadn't turned his head to the side just at that moment. The motion caught my attention and I moved toward him, frowning, wondering what in the world he was doing out here at this hour of the morning.

Early morning swim, I surmised, as I followed another curve in the vegetation. The field was clearly a natural boundary between the Baumgartner's timeshare and the one across the way. I wondered who the cabanas belonged to. I neared the edge of the field and stopped, my eyes widening and my stomach clenching.

Henry was leaning with his shoulder against one of the cabanas, peering around the side. His face was hidden from me, but I could clearly see his swim shorts pulled down, and his hand moving between his legs. Flushing, I began to back away, not wanting him to see me or even sense that I was there, fearing it was already too late. His head turned slightly back in my direction, and I instinctively ducked down and into the rushes. The ground there was moist and soft and I sank a little, giving me even more cover.

Now what? I didn't move for a moment, my heart beating fast, not daring to even breathe. Had he seen me?

What in the world would I say if he had? In all of the sexual scenarios I'd imagined since I knew I was coming back to see the Baumgartners, I had to admit that finding Henry masturbating on the beach had never crossed my mind.

Finally, I dared to poke my head up above the top of the grasses. He was still there, probably twenty feet away, and he was still...well, it was pretty clear what he was doing. His hand was still moving fast between his thighs—I could tell by the way his shoulder flexed—with his cheek resting against the side of the cabana. I was almost directly behind him now, instead of at an angle, and thankfully couldn't really see much anymore.

I stood there, indecisive, trying to figure out how to sneak away unnoticed, and it wasn't until he leaned a little further around the cabana that I wondered what it was he was looking at, what he was doing here in the first place, out here jerking off behind the old cabanas?

Too curious for my own good, I moved further into the rushes and shoregrass, pushing my way through slowly, trying not to make any noise. Henry was clearly too focused on what he was doing to hear me, I decided, as I found a better angle. My line of sight gave me a good view now of Henry from the side, his face twisted in pleasure, his hand gripping his cock—good god, he was big, like his father, the thick rise of his cock red and swollen, the head almost purple and clenched in his fist.

My pussy twitched at the sight of him, and I swallowed hard, telling myself I needed to get out of there—I needed to get out of there *now*. This was all kinds of wrong, and I didn't want to have any part of it. Maybe there was some woman he knew who sunbathed nude on the beach or something and he came down here to watch. Boys his age—what was he now, nineteen?—seemed to have no off switch when it came to arousal.

I told myself to go, to make my way back through the grass to the beach and run as fast as I could back the house. That's what I told myself, but when I saw the scene he was actually watching, I stood transfixed, unbelieving, paralyzed.

Brian was spread-eagle on a towel in the sand, Janie straddling him, both of them completely naked. He wasn't inside her of her—not yet. Her back was mostly to me, but I knew it was her, from the spill of her honey-colored hair over her shoulders to the Celtic tattoo in the small of her back that she'd shown off to Gretchen yesterday in the kitchen during dinner.

Brian's cock was in her hand and she stroked it between her ass cheeks as she rocked, obviously getting ready to fuck him. Staring, I moved further into the weeds, parting them so I could see better. Now I could see them almost from the side, Janie rubbing Brian's cock between her legs. He gripped her hips, his fingers digging into her flesh, his eyes half-closed. They were only about ten feet from the cabana where Henry was hiding watching…and about twenty feet, now, from where I was hiding…watching…

"Oh yeah!" I heard Brian's groan clearly as Janie slid him inside of her. I even heard her soft cry of surprise and pleasure, the sound carrying toward us downwind. Glancing at Henry, I saw his gaze on them, his cock hard in his hand as he watched his sister being fucked.

Had he followed them down here? Just stumbled across them? For a moment, I found myself angry that Brian and Janie were given so much freedom, that they were down here doing whatever they felt like on the beach in the first place—but I had to remind myself that they were grown-ups. Janie was drinking age now, for god's sake. Henry, too, was an adult. Mr. and Mrs. B. probably wouldn't care if their daughter had brought her boyfriend down to the beach for a little rendezvous… but what about their son's activities as he watched his sister getting fucked?

"Ohhhh yes, yes, Brian, harder!" Janie's voice carried again as she threw her head back, her breasts pointing skyward as she rocked on him. Brian had taken over most of the motion, though, his hips bucking her up and up, again and again. Christ, she was beautiful, her body pure perfection, a long, lean, tawny treasure, not a tan line in sight. I found myself wondering if Janie was shaved, like her mother, and the thought made me flush. I told myself it was from shame, but my pussy throbbed and I cupped my mound through my jeans to quell the ache a little.

I couldn't decide where to look—knowing I shouldn't be looking at any of it. Henry was stroking his cock faster now, biting his lip as he peered around the cabana, watching as his sister rode her boyfriend like he was some bucking bronco, Brian's hands cupping her breasts, kneading them in his hands. Janie leaned over him and pressed her breasts into Brian's face, giving both Henry and I a full view of her pussy taking the full length of her boyfriend's cock.

I suppressed a gasp and found myself wanting to get closer—god help me, I wanted to see. My hand rubbed unthinkingly between my legs, shoving the seam of my jean shorts up between my pussy lips, seeking the hard, aching button of my clit, looking for some sort of relief.

Then Brian was turning her over and Janie complied, getting up on her knees and arching her back, her bottom rising into the air like a cat that wants petting. He positioned himself behind her, his cock nice and slick and hard as he stroked it against her ass. Oh god, that was gorgeous. Simply stunning.

The little squeak that Janie let out when he entered her made my nipples tingle with longing, and I found myself slowly unzipping my shorts and sliding my hand inside for the second time that morning. I couldn't help it, apparently, any more than Henry could have. That's what I told myself as my fingers found my clit and began to rub it—that he'd stumbled across them and, like me, had been so surprised at first he couldn't move... and then... well... nature does take its course, and sometimes urges are so strong...

Henry's fist encircled his cock, pumping faster as he watched his sister now taking her boyfriend's cock doggie style, and I wondered how he could stay so quiet. His face clearly showed both his pleasure and his restraint—he didn't want them to know he was there, but he loved watching, was just as turned on as I was. And oh god, I was.

One hand crept up under my t-shirt, tweaking my nipple as I watched Janie getting fucked, her blonde hair hanging down over her face, her breasts swaying beneath her in the sand. The towel they'd been lying on had been forgotten in the heat of the moment as Brian pounded her hard from behind.

"Oh god, oh Janie, oh god baby I'm gonna—" Brian's warning brought an instant reaction from Janie, who shifted her hips quickly forward.

"Not inside!" She gasped, grabbing his cock and turning to start stroking and sucking him.

"Oh Janie, oh fuck." Henry's whisper made me shiver and I saw the first hot spurt of his cum erupt from the fat, purple head of his cock and explode like some twisted Rorschach against the back of the cabana wall. It was followed by another and another, his hips thrusting forward as he came, his head thrown back in a silent expression of pleasure.

The couple on the beach were too involved in what they were doing to hear him—or me, thankfully, for that matter. Janie was fingering her pussy as she sucked Brian off, and his hands were buried in her hair, shoving his cock deep into her throat. She'd clearly done that before. She could take almost his whole length, and watching it disappear into her mouth was beyond hot.

"Come on!" she urged, her voice thick as she took him out of her mouth to stroke him against her cheek. "Come all over me! Come on! Do it! Do it!"

"Ahhhhh god!" Brian's hips shifted forward and he did just as she asked, his cock jerking in her hand as he began to come, thick ropes of the stuff hitting her cheek and chin and breasts. I couldn't stand the tension for another minute, and my pussy spasmed with my own hot, shameful climax, my cheeks flushed and sweaty, my nipples hard and straining under my shirt.

Breathless, I sank to my knees in the soft ground, hidden in the rushes and glad for the cover. I couldn't believe what I'd just witnessed, what I'd just done. Was this me? Who was I? I thought I knew, but kneeling on the ground, my whole body still trembling from an incredible orgasm brought on by… good god, had I really just watched Janie and her boyfriend having sex…and had I really gone so far as to masturbate while I watched? Had I really just seen Henry watching his sister getting fucked, watched him jerk himself off…and found myself aching to put his cock in my mouth, feel it in my pussy?

Oh god.

When I finally caught my breath and dared to stand up and face the day—the sun had officially risen across the water—all of them were gone from the beach, as if it had never happened. Maybe I dreamed it, I told myself as I pushed my way out to the sand again and started walking slowly back down the beach toward the house. I wanted to believe it wasn't real, hadn't happened… of course I wanted to believe that. Because if it *had* happened…

Who did that make me? *What* did that make me?

I wasn't this girl… this woman. I wasn't. Was I?

I just didn't know anymore.

Chapter Six

"Come dance with me!" Gretchen grabbed me and pulled hard, making me yelp. My strawberry margarita sloshed over onto my hand and I licked at it as I stood.

"Where's Janie and Mrs...uhm, Carrie?" I was getting better at calling Mrs. B "Carrie" when she was around, but whenever I referred to her, my mouth still wanted to say "Mrs. B."

Gretchen pointed to the bar where the mother and daughter pair were ordering their own margaritas. We had agreed to this being a "girls night out," but Janie had stubbornly insisted on bringing Brian at the last minute, and Henry had tagged along, although he was too young to drink. I had no idea where Brian had disappeared to, but Henry sat across from me, arms crossed and frowning as he watched his sister at the bar.

"Want to dance, Henry?" I asked, reaching out my hand as Gretchen began to pull me toward the dance floor. He glanced up at me, his expression one of genuine interest for a moment, but then his attention shifted back to Janie and Mrs. B as they made their way toward the table.

"You go ahead!" He waved us on, and I didn't have much choice but to follow Gretchen—she was practically pulling my arm out of the socket. The music was live and totally Key West. The band was currently doing a cover of Jimmy Buffet's Margaritaville.

"Searching for my lost shaker of salt!" Gretchen's voice joined with the rest of the crowd as she pulled me close, sliding an arm around my waist and rocking me with her hips. It wasn't a fast or a slow song, really, hard to dance to, but Gretchen managed, and my body couldn't help but respond to hers as we swayed together. It seemed less about the dancing and music and more about the interaction between the audience and the band.

"Some people say that there's a woman to blame..." We sang together loudly, grinning as we changed the lyrics together, on cue. "But you know, it's your own damned fault!"

We laughed and Gretchen leaned in to whisper, "You look so hot in that..." as she slid a thigh between mine, pushing the black leather micro-mini she'd loaned me up to impossibly shameless heights. "Makes me want to take you into the little girls' room."

"You're bad," I said, but I was smiling as I turned, wrapping her arms around my waist and rubbing my behind against her front as we belted out another verse of Margaritaville.

"You two are already having too much fun." Carrie nuzzled up to both of us at once, kissing first Gretchen and then me on the cheek. "How are my girls?"

"I can't believe she's old enough to drink," I said, nodding toward the table where Janie was sitting beside her brother and sipping on a Margarita.

Carrie glanced over her shoulder at her daughter. "I know. She makes me feel old!"

"You're far from old." Gretchen's gaze swept over Carrie's outfit—unlike Gretchen, or me for that matter, her skirt wasn't outrageously short, but it was white leather, and it showed off the long, tanned expanse of her strong, shapely legs. Her blouse wasn't the midriff kind that Gretchen wore or the strapless kind that Gretchen had loaned me—just a short-sleeved navy silk, unbuttoned to a point that was just a little shy of inappropriate. She was dressed perfectly, as always—sexy, inviting, but not too slutty.

"Old enough to know better," Carrie said with a wink, sliding her hand down to the small of my back. "But still—"

"Too young to care." Gretchen and I both finished the sentence with her, and we all laughed.

"Mom, I want another one!" Janie sidled up behind us, holding her empty Margarita glass. "And Henry doesn't have any money."

"Take it easy, lightweight," I said, raising an eyebrow at her. "You do know there's tequila in those Margaritas, right?"

Janie rolled her eyes, but didn't answer me. "Mom?"

"Tell them to put it on my tab." Carrie nodded toward the bar. "Captain Tony knows me."

"Is that Captain Tony?" Gretchen asked.

"The one and only," Carried agreed.

I glanced toward the bar, where the bartender, wearing a goofy looking sailor's cap, was drawing a draught of beer. "Looks like a character."

Carrie laughed. "This is Key West—everyone's a character."

Janie was already talking to him and Captain Tony gave a nod in our direction before pulling another margarita glass out from under the bar.

"Has anyone seen Brian?" Carrie frowned, glancing around the bar. If the crowd dancing and milling around didn't make it impossible, the dimness made it truly too difficult to locate anyone.

"Bathroom?" Gretchen shrugged.

"Speaking of which…" I spotted the ladies' room in the far corner.

Gretchen smiled. "Want some company?"

"Not this time." I left the two of them together, weaving my way through. I gave Janie a smile on my way by, but she pretended she hadn't seen me.

The bathroom was small, and had clearly been converted from a one-person lavatory at some point— the outside door still locked, and there were two locking stalls painted pink inside, one handicapped, one not. I glanced in the full length mirror—the only mirror in the bathroom—noting again how short my skirt really was. Janie had made some nasty remark before we left about it, and it still stung, although the alcohol was making me feel a little more comfortable with its length.

Tonight I was determined to get Janie to come around, I decided, heading toward the small bathroom stall. That was my mission. I was hoping tonight's alcohol consumption was going to help me with that, too. I hurried, lifting my skirt and pulling down my panties before I'd even locked the stall door behind me. I was wiping and just about to flush when the outer door opened.

"We can't do it in here!" A hushed whisper and giggling.

"The door locks." A masculine voice this time—oh no. I heard the lock click and knew immediately what was about to happen. What was I supposed to do? Go out and excuse myself? Wait and sneak out after it was all over?

I decided to do the former, pulling up my panties and yanking down my skirt before reaching for the handle to flush, knowing the noise would announce my presence.

"Come here." The guy's voice again. "You know I always get what I want…and I want you."

Oh brother. I pushed the handle, but to my surprise, nothing happened.

"Brian, you're so bad." The girl's voice was low and teasing.

And the minute I heard the name 'Brian' I was alert, glad the toilet hadn't flushed. The last thing I needed tonight was Janie freaking out about me being in the bathroom she'd decided to fool around with her boyfriend in. I had to make peace with her somehow, and I was sure discovering her in a compromising position wouldn't help.

Of course, it wasn't like I hadn't seen them already, I thought, blushing at the memory. Not that *they* knew that… Okay, so I was stuck. I'd just wait it out, I decided, backing toward the corner of the stall.

"I can't believe I ran into you tonight!"

My brain registered the words, but the doubt had already surfaced. I knew Janie's voice, and that wasn't it. My mind had clearly wanted to believe it was—but the girl out there wasn't Janie. And if that was Brian…

Common name, I told myself. Could be it's not Janie's Brian. Right? Right.

Only one way to find out...

"We've only got a few minutes," Brian said.

It sounded like him. A *lot* like him. But I'd only really talked to him a few times, I told myself, craning my neck and trying to see them through the crack in the door. How could I be expected to know his voice? "Oh yeah, come on, gimme some of that..."

"Ohhh god, Brian, yes!"

They'd already started, the sound of their flesh slapping together loud in the closed space, the acoustics amplifying the noise. I leaned in closer to the crack in the stall door, determined to see if it was Janie's Brian, but even though I could see them both now, their were backs to me—he had her bent over a sink—and I couldn't determine for sure that it was him. Same hair color, sure. But there were lots of guys named Brian out there with dark hair... There was no mirror over the sink, so I couldn't see their faces. Had he been wearing a black t-shirt and jeans? I couldn't remember.

"Ohh god your pussy is sooo good!"

The girl moaned, gripping the sink. "Harder!"

It isn't Brian, I told myself, biting my lip and willing them to change positions so I could see for sure. I told myself I only wanted to see his face, but the sound of their sex was intoxicating, and I didn't want to admit I longed to see more. Her skirt was pushed up around her waist, her panties pulled down to her knees, but I could only see the smooth curve of her hip and the hard clench of his bare ass as he shoved himself inside of her.

Please don't be Janie's Brian, I thought, watching as his jeans slipped further down his thighs, giving me an even better view of the muscles flexing in his behind. God, that was good. I imagined being bent over the sink like that, being fucked from behind, hard and fast, feeling him filling me. Oh god, that was really, really wrong. Especially if that was Janie's Brian out there. *It isn't,* my mind insisted. *It just can't be.*

The last thing I wanted to have to do was tell Janie I'd seen her boyfriend fucking some girl in the bathroom. How exactly was I supposed to bring that up? I winced at the thought, shaking my head and praying it wasn't him. I didn't even want to acknowledge my reaction to it, how my pussy throbbed under the short cover of my skirt and my nipples hardened as I watched them fucking, harder, faster, more and more determined to reach their final, sweet destination.

Oh my god, what was *wrong* with me?

"Ohh fuck, you're gonna make me come!" He moaned and I shrank backward again, sitting down on the seat to wait for the finale, telling myself I didn't want to see, I didn't want to know, but oh god, my pussy was so achingly wet...

"Yes! Yes!" The redhead's voice was high and breathless, urging him on.

The whole room reverberated with the fast pounding of their flesh and I heard him moan loudly, the unmistakable sound of orgasm. I closed my eyes, biting my lip, trying not to hear the cries of pleasure or imagine that it was me spreading and arching and begging for that hot release of cum...

I tried hard to control my own breathing as I listened to the soft panting and fumbling of their post-coital readjustment.

"Will I see you back at the hotel tonight?" the redhead asked. Someone turned the sink on and I was relieved for the distraction, taking a few deep, steadying breaths.

"I'm here with that girl I told you about..." Now that his voice was back to "normal," I had a sinking feeling it really was Janie's Brian, but I still didn't want to believe it. He wouldn't do that to her... would he?

The girl sighed loudly. "Your parents still making you take her out?"

"Her parents are friends of my dad," Brian explained. "I can't say no."

They were going to leave, and I could just go back out there and pretend nothing had happened, I realized. I had no confirmation the guy out there was Brian. I tried peering through the crack in the door again, but his back was still to me.

"What about when you get back?" The redhead—I could see her face now, pouty and imploring—slid her arms around his waist.

"I'll give you a call when I get back to the hotel tonight." They kissed and I waited, wondering what to do. Janie should know, I told myself. If it's him, she should know. But did I really want to be the one to tell her?

"You promise?" the girl asked.

"Sure." He kissed her again. "Let's go."

It was my last chance. Did I want to know? Were they going to disappear into the crowd without any confirmation? Wouldn't that be a blessing after all?

Then I remembered—Brian's tennis shoes!

Ducking my head just enough, I looked under the stall door and saw them—a pair of black Karhu M1 running shoes with orange laces and stripes. Unmistakable. And I never would have noticed them at all if Doc hadn't cracked some joke about Brian's hundred-and-fifty-dollar Halloween shoes before we left!

Great. It really was Janie's Brian slipping out with some redhead he'd just bent over the bathroom sink. Some redhead he'd obviously been with before—back at the hotel. And I had to go tell her. Just great.

I slipped out of the stall and washed my hands at the sink, taking a long time in front of the dryer, not looking forward to what I had to do. I tried every way of approaching it I could possibly think of in my head as I stood there, and none of them seemed right.

I found Janie and Henry sitting at the table. Gretchen and Carrie were still dancing, and there was no sign of Brian. I decided to start with that.

"Have you seen Brian?" I asked, sitting next to Janie, addressing the question to her. I had to talk pretty loud to be heard over the music, and that concerned me. Maybe I should wait until we got back to the house?

She shrugged one shoulder, sipping her margarita, but didn't answer me.

"I thought..." I took a deep breath. "I mean...I saw him. By the bathroom. In the bathroom."

"Yeah, where is Brian?" Henry gave me a puzzled look and then glanced toward the bar but Janie pretended she hadn't heard his words at all.

"I don't know why you're so concerned about where he is," Janie snapped, finally turning to look at me. Her eyes, even in the dimness, flashed angrily. "I mean, what? Are you going down some list? My mom, Gretchen, probably even little Henry over here... do you want to fuck Brian, too?"

I actually sat back, gasping as if she'd punched me in the stomach, and it felt as if she had. I couldn't see anything as I got up from the table and pushed my way blindly toward escape. I heard Henry calling after me, but I didn't stop.

There were always cabs on the street in Key West—the cabbies made a fortune taking home people who'd had way too much to drink. And, judging from the kindly rastafarian's response, I'm sure it wasn't the first time some crying woman had jumped into his cab either.

I gave him the address of the Baumgartner's' timeshare and sat back as he pulled away, ignoring Henry calling my name as he burst out of the front door of Captain Tony's. I couldn't help my tears and just let them fall onto my bare thighs, staring out at the world passing by in a blur. I was going home to pack, call TJ, and go home, because Janie was right.

A week of experimentation when I was nineteen was different than a woman almost-thirty doing what I was doing. I couldn't go back—I wasn't that innocent, naïve girl anymore. I was turning into some wanton slut whose only motivation was, apparently, pure pleasure. Was that who I was?

No. Even if it meant losing TJ—my breath went away at the thought and it made me cry harder—this little reunion had to end before anyone got seriously hurt. I, for one, had been hurt more than enough.

I paid the cabbie when he pulled up at the house and just gave him a brief nod when he said, "Hope your night gets better," as I got out.

If I'd had my own room to run to, I think the whole thing would have ended then and there. I'm sure I would have locked the door, packed, and called TJ on my way to the airport before anyone even knew I'd gone.

But when I got into the house, Doc was sitting on the couch, drinking a beer and watching a movie. I stood in the doorway, hyper-aware of how awful I must look, and he frowned when he looked up and saw me. I couldn't help but think of the last time I'd come back to the house, a million years ago when I was just a kid, and found Doc alone. I couldn't help but remember, and I think he did, too.

He was holding me before I could speak, crossing the expanse of the room and pulling me into the circle of arms, whispering softness and kindness into my ears. "Ronnie, Ronnie, sweet Ronnie, it's okay, whatever it is, it's okay."

I didn't believe him, not really, but I wanted to, and instead of doing what I should have done, instead of pushing him away and running as far and fast as I could back to my life, my family, my husband, I wrapped my arms around his waist and sobbed against his shirt.

"I don't know what to do," I choked as he led me back toward the couch and pulled me into his lap. If I hadn't already felt transported back in time to the young, helpless girl I'd been, that would have done it. I rested my head on his shoulder as he rocked me and I cried.

"What is it?" he asked, pulling the tail of his shirt out to wipe at my tears. "Tell me. You can tell me."

"I feel like I'm doing everything wrong, "I sniffed. "Everyone seems to want something different from me, and I can't please everyone. I can't please *anyone!*"

He nodded, wiping my tears again—they wouldn't stop falling—and kissing my forehead. "Is this about you and TJ?"

I looked at him, frowning. "Carrie told you?"

"You're married, you know what it's like." He smiled softly. "Did you really expect her not to tell her husband?"

"I guess not." I shrugged, looking away, embarrassed now, wondering just how much he knew.

"He's not asking for more because you're not enough." His words made my breath stop.

I shook my head. "That makes no sense."

"If it was just sex, he'd go find it somewhere else, you know." Doc's eyes were dark as he looked at me and I remembered how I used to melt whenever he looked at me. "He wouldn't consult you at all."

I thought of Brian and the redhead in the bar. He was just a kid, of course—but cheating was cheating, right? Doc was right about that. If TJ wanted to... I frowned at the thought, shaking my head, trying to make sense of it.

"Sometimes we have so much love to give...it feels like we'll explode if we don't share it." Doc's words were soft and simple. He spoke as if he were explaining something to a child, and I felt like one.

"But...isn't it wrong?"

He smiled softly. "Do you think it's wrong?"

"It feels wrong." I sounded petulant and felt that way, too.

"Does it? Why?"

I shrugged. "Because I feel... guilty. Like I'm betraying my marriage."

"You can't betray your marriage if both of you agree that what you're doing isn't a betrayal," he replied simply.

I shook my head, swallowing hard around the lump in my throat. "Why does he want this? I don't understand..." I looked into his eyes, searching for answers there. "Why did you want *me?*"

"Because I loved you," he replied softly. "I wanted you because you were young and beautiful and I loved you."

"Well...I believe the first part, I guess... although I'm not young and beautiful anymore..." I frowned, remembering.

"Oh yes you are...both." He chuckled. "And I still love you."

"You love me?" I sighed. "Like, what? A daughter? A sister? A wife?"

"Like a lover." His thumb rubbed over my chin, making me shiver. "You loved me, too, you know."

Of course I had. I'd loved them both, and Gretchen too. I couldn't help it. But I was a kid then, and I was a grown-up now. Grown ups made choices. Grown ups narrowed their lives with choices—that was part of being a grown-up.

Doc spoke, almost as if he could read my thoughts. "When you have kids...you only have the one daughter, right?" I nodded. "Sometimes when you have another, you wonder if you're going to be able to love that child as much as the first. I loved Janie to pieces and thought I couldn't love another human being like that. It felt impossible. And then Henry came along, and he was just as amazing, but different, you know? You love them differently, because they're so unique, but it's still love. You find you have more than enough room in your heart for another. Your heart has an infinite capacity to love."

I understood the concept, but there was just one thing wrong with the theory. "But spouses aren't children."

"No," he agreed. "But the concept is the same, as long as you both agree that it's something you want. It's like anything in a marriage, you learn to negotiate and compromise. Are you telling me you don't want what he does?"

"I don't know." I squirmed in his lap, uncomfortable with the question, looking away.

He nudged my chin, turning my head back to him. "I think you do."

"Why do you think that?" I countered.

"Because your body wants it." His grip at my waist tightened and he slid his hand over my hip, pulling me closer. I felt, for the first time, how hard he was, and I flushed, my nipples tingling in response. "It's smarter than you are."

"Your body doesn't judge, Ronnie." His other hand moved in my hair, tilting my head back, feathering soft kisses at my throat. "Your head does that."

"Doc…" I swallowed, closing my eyes, feeling his hand moving down my hip, over my thigh. "I don't…"

"You're afraid, Ronnie." He pushed me from his lap and I gasped as he stood, towering over me. "You're afraid of losing him, but it's more than that. You're afraid of letting go, of losing control."

I stared at him, unable to speak.

"Come with me." He held out his hand.

I frowned. "Where?"

"Trust me."

That was the first step. Trembling, I took his hand and followed.

Chapter Seven

"Are you crazy?" I stood staring at Doc, mouth agape, as he put the raft on the sand at the water's edge and held out his hand to help me in. "I'm not getting in that thing!"

The water lapped at my bare feet—he'd insisted I remove my shoes before we even left the house—and a full moon made the waves look like watery crystals as they rode toward shore and crashed against the sand, leaving foamy lace behind.

"Trust me," Doc said again, reaching and grabbing hold of my hand this time. "Get in."

Sighing, I accepted his help into the boat, shrinking toward the side and waiting for him to get in, too. Then the raft moved on the sand and I shrieked, glancing backward in a panic at Doc, who pushed the inflatable into the water.

"What are you doing?!" I cried as he peeled off his t-shirt and tossed it onto the sand behind him, pushing the boat harder now as he waded in to his knees. "Don't leave me!"

He shook his head as the boat began to float, free of its lodging in the sand. "Did you really think I would push you out there and leave you?"

I frowned, trying to ignore the pounding of my heart, as he pulled himself over the rounded yellow edge of the inflatable—the water was up to his chest now—and swung a leg over. He settled in across from me with a smile.

"Okay?" he asked, taking an oar in each hand and beginning to row.

I didn't answer, glancing back toward shore, watching it slowly disappear as I considered his question. Was I okay? Since I'd begun this journey down memory lane with the Baumgartners, I'd felt uneasy, off-kilter. The world, which had once felt so safe and solid, had somehow tilted sideways and I was struggling to keep my footing—and I was afraid to look down to see what was waiting for me, should I fall.

"Where are we going?" I asked, turning back to watch Doc rowing, the oars slicing through the moonlit waves, his shoulder muscles flexing as each stroke took us further and further away from shore…from safety.

"Do you trust me?"

Of course I did. The man had been a little like a second father to me as a teen, and had transformed into an experimental lover during my young adulthood. He was kind, wise, and he loved me. I knew it was true…but being alone out here on the water, so far from shore, made me uneasy still. I wasn't afraid of Doc, I knew that much. But what was I afraid of?

"Ronnie, do you trust your husband?"

Slowly, I nodded. I did, I always had, and he had proven himself to be trustable again and again. Thinking about TJ made me miss him suddenly, deeply, and I longed to hear the sound of his voice, to feel the rake of his whiskers over my cheek.

Doc stopped rowing, letting the boat drift. The waves rocked us gently up and down and we sat in the silence, looking at each other in the moonlight.

"What are you afraid of?" he asked, leaning toward me as he asked the question—the same question I'd been asking myself. It was just a two person raft, and when he moved, our crossed-knees touched. "Tell me."

"I…" Shifting my weight made the boat rock. I steadied myself, shaking my head. "I don't know."

"Don't you?" Doc grabbed the oars again and gave a strong, solid pull, sending us moving swiftly through the water again and making me gasp. "Are you afraid now?"

"Yes," I admitted, swallowing hard and glancing back toward shore. We were so far! The windows in the house were just tiny squares painted on the night. "But I don't know why."

"You love TJ, don't you?"

I nodded. "Of course I do."

"Has he ever given you a good reason not to trust him?"

He hadn't. I mean, aside from a few things here and there—saying he'd do something and putting it off, small promises made not kept. But in the scheme of things, throughout our marriage? "No."

"Does he lie to you?"

I shook my head. "No."

"Does he cheat on you?"

I hesitated then. We'd talked about being with other people, and now I had officially betrayed our marriage, twice, with his permission. But to my knowledge, he'd never cheated. He'd expressed an interested, yes, but technically…"No."

Doc took my hands, looking into my eyes. His were dark and wet with reflected moonlight. "Do you really believe he would steer you wrong?"

"Not on purpose, I guess…" I bit my lip, thinking. "I'm just afraid he's going to…well, like this…" I looked around us, at how far out we are, feeling the waves rocking the raft. I wasn't stupid—I understood Doc's metaphoric little boat trip perfectly. "What if he rows us out too far… or does something stupid, like throwing away our oars."

"What if he does?" He squeezed my hands in his. "Would you trust him anyway?"

"I…" Frowning, I pulled away, shaking my head. "Why should I have to?"

"Love is trust," Doc whispered, and the words were so soft the might just have been waves lapping at the sides of the boat.

I folded my arms across my chest—I was still wearing the spaghetti-strapped top and mini-skirt, and while the night was warm, the water made it feel cooler. "Why should I have to prove anything?"

"Why should he?" Doc countered with a wise smile.

I gave up, feeling tears pricking my eyes. "I just…I don't want to lose him. I don't want to lose what we have."

"Do you think he does?"

"No," I admitted softly. TJ loved me, I knew that. He didn't want to lose me or our marriage, any more than I did.

"Then trust him," Doc urged, reaching over to wipe away one of my tears with his thumb and lifting my chin, making me look into his eyes. "Let your heart lead you. Not your fear. Not your guilt. Not your shame."

His words made so much sense and I felt myself melting, "Doc..."

"Trust him to steer the boat." He leaned forward and kissed my wet cheek.

"But..."

Doc sighed, leaning back and snapping one of the oar holders open. "No buts, Ronnie. None. Not even if he throws away the oars." He snapped the other open and my heart plummeted.

"What are you doing?!"

Doc gave each oar a shove and they were free, floating lazily away. "Throwing away the oars."

"Are you crazy?" I panicked, grabbing over the side for one and just succeeding in getting myself wet. It was already out of reach! "What now?"

"That's a great question." Doc smiled, leaning back, and I marveled at his calm. "Are you afraid?"

I looked back and forth between the oars as they disappeared into the darkness. "Yes!"

"But do you trust me?"

I stared at him, angry, confused, afraid...but still... "Yes."

"Then come here." He held his arms out to me and I shook my head, but my body knew better than I did and I went to him, letting him pull me against his chest. He was warm, solid, and I took a shaky breath as the boat rocked us further and further from shore.

"Deep breaths," Doc encouraged, kissing my hairline and using the rise and fall of his chest to instruct me. "Relax."

I groaned, closing my eyes against the distance between us and land. "I can't do this."

"Yes you can," he murmured, his hand moving down my back, seeking the expanse of bare skin between my skirt and shirt and rubbing there. "Just let go and trust. That's all you have to do."

I kept my eyes closed, trying not to think, trying to keep my mind from racing to all the scary, looming thoughts, all the what ifs... Instead, I rested my head against Doc's chest, feeling the gentle rock of the raft, listening to the steady beat of his heart with my own.

"That's good..." His hands moved under my shirt now and I didn't stop him as he stroked my back, petting me. "I can feel you relaxing..."

I was. In spite of my fear, which still had my heart beating hard, I couldn't help but be calmed by his voice, his touch. I found myself softening, letting myself go. Doc shifted his weight and me with him as he moved, letting me feel his erection, hard against my hip.

"Let your body lead you..." He whispered against my ear, giving me shivers. "Your head thinks it knows, but it doesn't..." His hands moved around the front now, still under my shirt. I wasn't wearing a bra—I still didn't really need one—and he cupped my breast, squeezing gently. "Your body knows what it wants..."

I moaned softly when he thumbed my nipple, feeling a sweet tingle between my thighs. I wanted to stop him—no, that wasn't quite true. I felt like I should stop him. Something kept telling me it was wrong, this man wasn't my husband, I shouldn't want... I shouldn't...

"So sweet..." Doc had my shirt pulled up and my nipple in his mouth so fast I could barely take a breath. I wiggled in his lap, gasping, my hands gripping his shoulders, not sure if I wanted to push him away or pull him closer. Where was there to go, anyway?

I opened my eyes briefly, seeing the faint lights at the shore, and my belly lurched with sudden fear.

"Stop thinking," Doc insisted, pushing me back in the raft, so I was leaning against the opposite side. "Just feel."

"But—" The protest died on my lips when he pushed my skirt up and pulled my panties aside, pressing his fingers there first, plunging deep enough to make me gasp, and then dipping his head down to taste me with his tongue. "Ohhh!"

My clit throbbed in his mouth as he sucked and licked me with an eager hunger than soon had me spreading wider, silently asking for more. There wasn't a lot of room in the little raft, but I lifted my hips for his tongue, his fingers, digging my heels into the bottom of the raft.

"Oh please," I begged, rubbing my own nipples through my shirt, pushing the feeling further, further, needing more. "Oh god!" All thought had gone, and there wasn't any more fear or hesitation. I let him—I let myself. I couldn't stop it and didn't really want to. That was my secret, guilty admission. I wanted this, had always wanted this, and denying it took infinite more work than acknowledging my own self-confession.

"Good girl!" Doc chuckled when I threw first one bare leg and then the other over the side of the boat, spreading wide and lifting my hips up for his straining tongue. His hands slid under my skirt, gripping my clenched ass, pulling me against his greedy mouth. The sensation was almost too much to bear.

"Don't stop," I whispered, but I knew he wouldn't. His tongue lashed at my clit, again, again, and my thighs trembled as I felt my orgasm coiling low in my belly, waiting to spring. I moaned when he sucked at my clit, as if it were a little cock, trying to suck it deep into his mouth. That made me arch further, my head going back against the side of the raft.

"Gonna... ohhhh... god... Doc, please!" My warning made him even hungrier and I couldn't hold it back, feeling my climax already beginning, making me quiver. I was lost, found, instantly transported and taken, the sweet throb of my clit in his wet mouth beyond sweetness, beyond love.

"Oh god, oh god," I whispered again and again as he slowly let me settle back into the boat. My head still hung off the back of the raft and I gasped, opening my eyes and seeing the moon floating above us in a sea of stars, the water below reflecting its face in a distorted white ribbon of moonlight on a black ocean.

When I lifted my head to look at him, sitting back against the opposite side of the boat again, his suit discarded, his cock in his hand, he was like a glowing, silver god in the moonlight, and I couldn't resist.

"Oh yesss," he moaned as I knelt between his thighs and took his cock into my hand, my mouth. I instantly remembered the taste and feel of him, the weight of his balls cradled in my hand. I'd been such a young, naïve girl then, so unsure but willing to learn. Very teachable, oh yes, definitely that.

I'd learned a lot since the last time Doc and I had been together.

"Oh Christ!" His hips bucked as my tongue made fat, flat sweeps around the head of his cock, pausing to give a little extra attention to the sweet spot, flicking back and forth at the frenulum. My fingernails—never anywhere near as long as Mrs. B's, but still long enough to do the job—scratched lightly over his balls as I sucked him in, my nose pressed into the dark thatch of his pubic hair.

Then I really showed him what I could do, working his cock with my mouth and hand at once, nice short even strokes that had him swelling nicely in my hand, his breath beginning to match my pace. Whenever I felt his cock twitch, that gentle, telltale throb, I'd take him deep and hold him there, using my tongue to press him against the roof of my mouth until his breathing slowed a little. And then I'd begin again, those sweet, short strokes, making soft, hungry noises in my throat as I sucked him.

"Ahhhhh baby, wait," he finally groaned, grabbing my hair and pulling my head back. "I want to fuck you."

I wanted it, too. Unzipping my skirt, I slid it and my panties down and tossed them with his suit on the floor of the raft. Doc lifted my shirt and pulled it off as I straddled him, rubbing his cock between my swollen pussy lips. His eyes were dark as his gaze swept over me in the moonlight and his hands followed, cupping my breasts and tweaking my nipples as I jerked him against my clit.

"Put it in," he murmured, shifting his hips. "I want—ohhhhh god!"

I was wet enough to take him in without any resistance and our hips met as I slid down all the way to the base. Giving a little whimper, I made little circles in his lap, feeling his cock moving deep inside me. His hands moved from my breasts to my hips, rocking me back and forth, his fingers digging in as we fucked.

"Faster," he urged, lifting me upward as he slid deeper into the raft, so his head was resting on the floor. I did what he asked, leaning forward and grabbing onto the edge of the inflatable raft, rocking faster, taking him deeper with every thrust. Doc found my nipples with his tongue, sending sweet waves of pleasure down to my aching clit.

His hands moved over my ass, spreading me wider as he began to take over the movement, thrusting up into me, his tongue still bathing my nipples in saliva. I was so close I could barely keep myself from coming, but I wanted it to last and last, the sweet swell of his cock inside of me, the hard pounding of his hips against mine.

"Oh Ronnie... baby..." I knew the sound in his throat, that low growl, telling me he was about to come. I ground my hips against his, feeling the boat rocking faster with our motion, making me dizzy. I closed my eyes and slid my hand down between us, searching through the wetness for the aching bud of my clit, needing just a little nudge to push me over the edge.

"Ahhhhhhhhh!" He groaned and thrust deep, shuddering beneath me, and the sound and feel of his climax sent me over. I trembled in his arms, feeling the pulse of his cock as my own orgasm overtook me, my pussy clenching and releasing as I came.

"Oh Doc," I whispered, as he pulled me close and I shivered, cold now in the night air, our bodies covered with a sheen of sweat. "Oh... oh..."

"So beautiful," he murmured, kissing my cheek, my chin, my mouth, as he rolled to his side and tucked me into the raft beside him, our limbs entangled. His fingers moved through my hair as we kissed, lost in the moment, and I wondered if he was remembering, too, the first time we'd been together alone like this.

"Good as you remembered?" I whispered, tilting my head back so I could look into his eyes.

He smiled. "Better."

Suddenly, I sat up, looking around us in the darkness. "Doc! How are we going to get back! We're so far!" I pointed toward the shore, the house a faint light in the distance.

"Didn't I ask you to trust me?" Doc chuckled as he sat up, reaching over the side of the boat. I watched as he miraculously produced an oar and snapped it into place. He did the same on the other side.

"Velcro," he explained, leaning over and kissing the tip of my nose. "There's always a spare set."

"So we were safe the whole time?" I sat back, incredulous.

He cocked his head at me and smiled. "What do you think?"

The metaphor wasn't lost on me, and I smiled, quiet as I began to pull my clothes back and Doc started to row us back toward shore.

* * * *

My heart sank when I saw Henry sitting on the beach as Doc pulled the raft the last few feet in to shore. Had he followed me? Or was everyone back, I wondered, my gaze moving toward the windows in the house, looking for signs of movement. That's when I noticed he wasn't alone.

"Hey, Dad, I thought we weren't supposed to take the raft out at night?" Henry called.

Doc pulled the raft toward the house. "Special circumstances."

"Are you okay?" Henry grabbed my hand as I walked by, stopping me short. I didn't want to talk. I most definitely didn't want to be introduced to the girl who was sitting on the blanket next to him.

"I'm fine," I replied, trying to shake him loose, but his grip was too tight. "Is everyone home?"

"I don't know." He shrugged. "Liz gave me a ride back here so we could go for a swim." Neither of them were wet or wearing suits but I wasn't about to mention that fact. I wanted to get into the house as fast as I could.

"Hi, I'm Liz." The redhead waved and gave me a smile and I tried to smile back. It was the same redhead from the bar, the one Brian had bent over the bathroom sink. This day just kept getting better and better…

"Hi, Liz," I replied, pulling my hand from Henry's persistent grip. "You two have fun."

Right. Now what? I wondered as I walked through the sand toward the house where Doc was securing the raft. Janie's boyfriend was cheating on her…with the same girl Henry happened to bring home? I had better odds winning the lottery than finding myself in this predicament, I thought, glancing back at the two of them sitting close, holding hands.

"You okay?" Doc asked as I approached, reaching for my hand.

"Sure," I agreed, letting him take my hand before we went into the house. "I just need a shower."

"Want me to join you?" He raised an eyebrow, smiling.

I smiled back. "Not this time."

I needed time to think.

Turning the water as hot as I could stand it, I stood under the spray and wondered what to do. Should I tell Janie? Should I warn Henry? Or should I just stay out of it and let it all crumble down around their heads like it clearly, inevitably would.

I realized, as I got out of the shower and pulled on a t-shirt and comfortable pair of shorts, that at least Janie and Henry's problems had distracted me from my own for a while.

I heard Mrs. B and Gretchen laughing as I made my way downstairs and knew they, at least, had returned. When I poked my head around the banister, I found everyone sitting around—Doc and Mrs. B and Gretchen cuddled on the couch, Janie and Henry next to each other on the loveseat, and Henry and the redhead sitting on the floor. I surveyed the scene for a moment, blinking back my surprise as another round of laughter went through the group, brought on by something Gretchen said.

"I told her three times!" Gretchen howled, leaning against Carrie as she doubled over in laughter. "And *she did it anyway!*"

"Some people," Liz remarked, smiling.

"There she is!" Carrie smiled warmly as I came slowly down the stairs, still incredulous. Obviously Janie didn't know about the redhead, or she'd be freaking out, right? Still, the redhead knew about her…that much had been clear from the bathroom encounter…but she didn't care? And Brian, he sat back, his arm thrown casually around Janie's shoulder, cool as could be. He didn't care that the redhead was now clearly interested in Henry?

The complexity of it made my head spin.

"Come sit," Carrie implored, patting the couch between herself and Gretchen. I contemplated that idea for a moment, but then saw Janie's cool gaze out of the corner of my eye.

"I think I'm going to get something to drink," I replied, redirecting myself toward the kitchen.

"Ooooo good idea!" Liz agreed, jumping up. "More margaritas! I'll help!"

Great.

Before I knew it everyone was crowding into the little kitchen, the blender going at full tilt with tequila and margarita mix.

"But Daddy, you said you liked this one," Janie teased, turning and pulling her shirt up in back, and her skirt down to reveal the top of her panties—Hello Kitty—and then pulled those down to expose her tattoo.

"Tramp stamp," Henry muttered behind me, and Liz, the redhead, giggled.

"I guess, as tattoos go, it's not bad," Doc said with a grimace. "I'm just saying, it seems like everyone has so *many* of them nowadays."

"I've got four," Liz piped up. "Bet you can't guess where."

Henry's eyes turned to her with interest and I smiled to myself.

Then Brian spoke up, "I bet I can."

The words, *"Not fair, that's cheating,"* almost slipped off my tongue as Janie turned and nudged him with her elbow. But she was smiling, teasing. I flushed and slipped past Brian and the redhead toward the door, excusing myself.

At least the upstairs bathroom was quiet and I could think. I splashed water on my face to cool it and stood at the sink for a minute, wondering what to do next. Clearly I couldn't say anything to Janie. Or Henry, either. How could I? Then again... how could I not? My stomach clenched at the thought, and I took a deep breath and opened the door, choking off a cry of surprise at Brian standing outside.

"Sorry, didn't mean to scare you," he apologized and I found myself looking down at his shoes—those black tennis shoes with the orange stripes and laces. Unmistakable.

The words were out of my mouth before I'd even thought about it. "Did you tell them you knew Liz had a tattoo of some Chinese character on her left butt cheek?"

He stared at me for a moment, the slight widening of his eyes the only indication he gave of registering what I'd said.

"What about the angel wings on her shoulder?" I prompted him, raising my eyebrows, waiting. "Did you tell them about those?"

"Liz knows about Janie," Brian said with a shrug, leaning against the door frame. "She doesn't care."

"But Janie obviously doesn't know about Liz," I snapped.

He shrugged again. "So?"

"Well, it looks like Liz has turned her interest elsewhere anyway." I gave him a smug smile.

"That little moron?" Brian snorted. "She's just stringing him along. Probably trying to make me jealous. Whatever."

"What if I tell Janie?" I asked, glaring at him. "What then?"

"So what if you do?" Brian rolled his eyes. "You think she'll break up with me over that? Please. She'll forgive me in a heartbeat, and I'll be banging her again inside two weeks, bet me on it. Girls like her...it's too easy."

Girls like her... what did that mean?

"You should be ashamed of yourself."

He rolled his eyes. "Whatever, lady."

"Do you really care so little about her?"

He shrugged. "She's all right, I guess. Gives good head."

I wanted to hit him. I might have, if Henry hadn't hauled him into the hallway and punched him in the face. It all happened so fast I barely had time to catch my breath. Henry was yelling and swinging, Brian was yelling and swinging back, although more half-heartedly, since he hadn't expected the attack. Doc came roaring up the stairs to break it up, pushing each of them against an opposite wall with the heel of each hand.

"What the hell is going on here?"

"Ask Brian." Henry spat, wiping blood from his lower lip and glowering. "Or Ronnie can tell you. Tell them, Ronnie."

"I...don't..." I stood there with my mouth open, paralyzed, my heart sinking when I saw Janie standing at the top of the stairs with Liz beside her, Gretchen and Carrie crowding in behind them.

"Well, whatever it is..." Doc frowned, looking between the two still struggling boys and then back to me. "I think we should call it a night."

Janie howled, turning to her mother and sobbing. "This is all her fault! Why did you ask her to come back? I hate her!"

I winced at her words, shrinking back against the bathroom door. She glared at me, her eyes flashing, as she hissed, "I hate you! *I hate you!*" before running to her room.

Brian shook Doc off, heading toward the stairs, mumbling a quick good night, and before I could register what had happened, both he and Liz were gone, Henry had locked himself in his room, and Doc, Carrie and Gretchen had settled back downstairs on the couch. The TV was on, and Carrie had invited me to join them, but I gave her a shaky "No thanks" reply. The couch bed was technically my bedroom, but I didn't want to hang out there, so I went to Gretchen's room—my old bedroom—stretched out on the bed, and cried myself to sleep.

Chapter Eight

The water was so warm and buoyant I could have floated forever, the sun bright behind my eyes as the waves gently rocked me. I was, strangely, more relaxed than I'd been since I arrived. Just being out in the water reminded me of what I'd termed the "raft therapy session" I'd had with Doc the night before, and the memory made me feel warm from the inside out. Something had broken open in me then, and I had no more qualms about being here. TJ was due to fly in soon—just a few more days—but I wasn't worried anymore. Things would work out.

I'd decided that was going to be my mantra for the rest of this little vacation. Things would work out. Whatever was going on with Janie...well, it would work itself out. If Brian was cheating on Janie, well...it would work itself out. If Henry was interested in the girl Brian had been cheating with, well...that would work itself out, too. Somehow.

I opened my eyes and started swimming toward shore, my sudden hunger outweighing my craving for sun. I grabbed my towel off the sand and went into the house, shivering at the sudden cold—the air conditioning was running full blast against the incredible heat of the day. I grabbed a banana off the counter and ate it on my way up the stairs, heading for the shower.

I was alone in the house—everyone had decided to go for ice cream, but I'd decided I didn't want to be in the same car with Janie. Even if I wanted to believe it was all going to work out, I didn't think I needed to put myself in harm's way or volunteer for any further abuse. And I knew, just from the way Janie bristled when I came downstairs that morning after spending the night in Gretchen's room—without Gretchen, incidentally, who had given me a sheepish smile when she came out of the Baumgartner's bedroom in the morning—that Janie was still angry about the night before.

So I didn't expect Henry to be in the bathroom. I probably would have just opened the door without even thinking, but I caught a glimpse of him in the mirror through the crack in the door—it was slightly ajar. He was standing there completely naked, his cock hard in his hand, with a pair of pink panties pressed to his face.

I knew they were panties, because I recognized the "Hello Kitty" on them—Janie had been wearing them last night when she'd shown us her tattoo. Frozen, I stood there and watched as he lazily stroked himself, eyes closed, totally oblivious to my presence. He inhaled deeply, groaning softly, his hand moving faster up and down his cock.

I shrank back, my stomach clenching, afraid he'd find me here watching him. But I didn't turn and go. I didn't. I couldn't figure out why Henry was home—he'd left with everyone else to get ice cream, I thought. He knew I was out swimming... maybe he'd come back to have some time alone? *To do...this?* I stared as he wrapped the panties around the base of his cock, stroking himself now with the silky material.

He's a young man, I reminded myself, swallowing hard. A wind blows and they get hard. It's biological. But those were Janie's panties. His *sister's* panties. That was just...wrong. All kinds of wrong. And still, I didn't move. I didn't barge in and ask him just what in the hell he thought he was doing. I didn't turn and walk away. I stood in the doorway and watched, feeling an ache swelling between my legs. I didn't move until Henry stopped, giving a quick, guilty look toward the door, and then moved to open it. Quickly, as silently as I could, I slipped into Gretchen's room and hid behind the door.

I peeked between the crack in the door and saw him head to his room. He pushed the door open and then swung it behind him, but it didn't latch. Now what? I knew I should just go take a shower and pretend nothing had happened, but somehow I couldn't. The memory of him standing behind the cabana, watching his sister be fucked... and now this, seeing him masturbating with a pair of his sister's panties... what was going on?

I crept down the hall, just inches at a time. His door was open, just slightly ajar and I stopped there with a good view of Henry stretched out on his bed, his fist pumping his cock with furious enthusiasm. I stood there, undecided, knowing what he was doing was wrong—and what I was doing was even more wrong. But I couldn't stop.

My god, he was beautiful. He was like a younger version of Doc, tall and broad and tanned, like some gorgeous Greek god, his dark hair tousled and a little too long, hanging over his forehead. His cock...oh no, I shouldn't be thinking it, should most definitely not be wanting it like I was... such a gorgeous thing, standing straight up, the pink panties making the red tip of his cock look even darker.

"Ohhhh yeah," Henry moaned, squeezing his fist tight, and I saw a slow, sweet seep of pre-cum flow out onto his sister's panties. "Oh god, Janie, suck me, baby, suck it good..."

My belly tightened at his words. Knowing he had his sister's panties was one thing—I mean, even I could rationalize that in some way. The smell of pussy was...well...intoxicating. But knowing that he was actually fantasizing about Janie, picturing her sucking his cock? That was something else altogether.

And still I didn't go. Instead, I found my hand pressed between my legs, cupping my aching mound as I watched him. The head of his cock played peek-a-boo with the satin of his sister's panties. The glistening tip wept continually, soaked up by the silky material that grew darker and darker with every pump of Henry's hand.

"Yeah, I want your pussy," he murmured, his head going from side to side, his hips thrusting up. "Spread it. Oh god yeah. Fuck me, Janie. Yeah!"

Oh god. This was so wrong. My fingers slipped under the wet crotch of my suit, seeking the heat of my pussy, watching as Henry reached next to him on the night table for a bottle of baby oil. Mrs. B had a ton of the stuff around to use for tanning...but this clearly wasn't the first time Henry had done this. He let several fat drops fall onto the naked head of his cock before putting it back on the table.

"Oh god, you're so tight," he groaned as he eased his cock through the tight press of his fist. With his other hand he brought her panties to his face again and inhaled the scent of her deeply. "Janie...Janie...ohhhh..."

I bit my lip, watching as he began to thrust, knowing he was picturing Janie on top of him, imagining his cock pressing deep into his own sister's pussy. It was wrong, it was downright wicked, but it was soooo hot...just the thought of it made my fingers soaked with my juices and I spread them through my pussy lips, focusing on my aching clit.

"Fuck me, Janie!" he begged, growling and thrusting and reminding me so much of Doc with every motion. It was both eerie and exciting. Henry might have been imagining shoving his cock into his sister's pussy—but I was imagining him in mine. I wanted to climb up and ride him, god help me, I really did. That hard cock was so hard to resist...

"Oh yes yes yes, Sissy, make me come!"

My eyes widened—I hadn't heard Henry call Janie "Sissy" in years, but here it was, coming out of his mouth just as he was about to climax, whispering it over and over, "Sissy, yes, Sissy, yes, Sissy, yesssss," as he imagined fucking her deep and hard. I rubbed my clit faster, unable control myself, my breath coming fast as I watched.

"Oh fuck me! Now! Ohhhhh!" Henry's cock exploded, thick jets of cum spilling over his tight glistening, pumping fist, sliding down toward the thick, dark nest of his pubic hair. He rubbed Janie's panties over the head of his cock, groaning, his cum splashing the sly, wide-eyed kitten appliqué, soaking the material.

Seeing him come sent me soaring and I pressed my flushed face against the doorframe, shuddering with my climax. My pussy throbbed, aching for the thrust of a cock, my nipples hard and straining against my suit. I bit my lip to keep from making any noise, backing away from the door, afraid he might hear or sense my orgasm somehow.

"Oh god," I heard him whisper.

The reality of what he'd been doing—what *I'd* been doing—sank in, and I crept shamefully away, sneaking down the stairs, avoiding the places where they creaked, and went back out onto the beach, where I'm sure he thought I still was.

I spread out a towel and stretched out on my back, throwing an arm over my eyes against the heat of the sun, and wondered what I was going to do. *It will all work out.* Right. That was my new motto. I tried not to remember Henry holding his sister's panties to his nose, tried not to remember him pretending to fuck his sister's pussy as he came...

I heard the door wall and, while I didn't look up, my whole body tensed in anticipation. I was glad of the heat, hoping it would explain the flush in my cheeks.

"Hey Ronnie."

I uncovered but shaded my eyes. "Hey, Henry... what flavor did you get?"

He stopped, cocking his head at me and frowning. "Huh?"

"Ice cream," I reminded him.

"Oh." He smiled, sitting next to me. He was wearing a bathing suit now, but I couldn't help remembering him without one... I tried, but I really couldn't help it. "I didn't go."

"How come?"

"Didn't feel like it." He shrugged, looking thoughtful, letting sand sift through his fingers. "I guess I'm mad at Janie."

"Janie?" I sat up on my elbows, eyeing him. "And here I thought you'd be mad at Brian...or...Liz..."

"She deserves better than him." He scowled. "They both do."

"Well, I have to agree with you there."

Henry made a fist, gripping the sand in his hand. "He's such an asshole."

I nodded. "Again, all kinds of agree over here..."

He looked over at me and smiled. "Wanna go for a walk?"

"Sure." I stood, brushing sand off, and he did the same. The sand was hot and we walked, barefoot, down to the water's edge where it was cool and wet.

"Aren't you mad at Liz?" I asked.

"No." Henry shrugged, reaching over and grabbing my hand. "She just got caught up in Brian's little web."

"And your sister didn't?"

He frowned, swinging my hand as we walked. "I warned her about him."

"You mean... after last night?" I winced, imagining that confrontation.

"No, before," he replied. "Before you came."

I noticed we were walking around the shore grass again, and remembered with a flush the last time I'd come this way. "How did you know?"

"I just knew."

"It's sweet that you're so protective of her..." I bit my lip, hesitant, not sure how to bring it up but sure I had to, somehow. "But Henry...I think you might...be a little too...attached, I guess...to your sister..."

He frowned, stopping to look at me. "What do you mean?"

"I just think...I think..." I bit my lip again, trying to think of what to say, how to say... "Well, I think you need a girlfriend, that's what I think."

He laughed, swinging my hand as we started to walk again. "Are you volunteering?"

"I was thinking someone more your age..." I said, rolling my eyes. "Someone not married."

Henry snorted. "That doesn't mean anything around here."

"What do you mean?" We were coming up on the old cabanas again, and the memory of Henry masturbating behind them, his cock squeezed in the very hand that now held mine, made me flush.

Henry shrugged. "My parents... and Gretchen... and you... and... whoever..." I was the one to stop this time, gaping at him. "We're not stupid, you know."

"When did...how...?" I shook my head, not wanting to believe it.

Henry's smile was slow and a little mischievous. "Janie and I both saw you, that summer."

"Oh Henry..." I reached out and touched his cheek. "I'm so sorry."

He shook his head. "My parents have always been very...open."

"How open?" My antennae went up and I frowned as I sat down in the sand, facing the water, and he did, too.

"Well, their marriage is obviously open." He started playing in the sand again, writing his name, erasing it.

"Henry...has anyone ever...I mean..." I swallowed, wondering if I wanted to know. "No one ever abused you, did they?"

He turned to me, wide-eyed. "No!"

"I just wondered...because...well..." I looked out at the water, the sun brilliant on its surface. "I saw you, too."

"What do you mean?" He resumed writing his name in the sand.

"Upstairs in your room..." I said, clearing my throat. "With Janie's panties." Oh god. Just the thought made me blush. "And before...right here, by the cabanas..."

He didn't look at me, but I heard him whisper. "Oh fuck."

"She's your *sister.*" I did look at him, then, at the flush in his cheeks, his eyes downcast.

"I know…" He sighed. "But…I can't seem to help it."

I took a deep breath and just asked. "Did anything ever happen between you and Janie?"

He shrugged, brushing his hands together to get the sand off. "When we were kids, we played around. Not anything major. Just pretending kissing and stuff. I think maybe every brother and sister might do something like that."

I didn't know. I had a sister, but I didn't have a brother. Still, if I had a brother who looked like Henry…

"But god, Ronnie, she's gotten so…" Henry's eyes moved over my suit and I could almost feel the heat of his gaze. I pretended not to notice.

"Grown up?" I suggested

"You could say that…" He laughed softly. "And she's constantly flaunting it around the house…*constantly*…it's enough to drive me crazy!"

I smiled, taking his hand and squeezing it. "You *really* need a girlfriend."

"Sure you're not volunteering?" he asked again, his eyes dark, so like Doc's, full of a deep, greedy hunger, an unstoppable lust…

"Stop…" I whispered as he let go of my hand, slowly encircling my wrist and sliding his palm up my forearm.

"Do you really want me to?" he murmured, his fingers grazing my shoulder, my collarbone, trailing down toward the V of my suit.

"No." I answered honestly, closing my eyes when his finger touched my hard nipple through the material.

"Really?" he asked, pressing his mouth right next to my ear.

"Really," I breathed, sliding my arms around his neck and letting him kiss me. It was wrong, but I wanted it, and he did too. I rationalized that it was better this, better me, than Janie. Living without boundaries clearly had consequences, I thought, and maybe this boundary was better crossed than another, more taboo one...

"Wait," he murmured, leaving me there and running over to one of the cabanas. He produced a blanket which he spread out on the sand, urging me to get on it. I crawled to the center and laid down on my back, seeing his eyes darken as he looked down at me.

"Oh Henry," I moaned when he pressed me back into the sand, his thigh between mine. I could feel his cock, hard and ready even though he'd come just half an hour before. I wanted to reach for it but restrained myself, letting him explore me first. He sat up between my legs, his erection obvious, tenting his shorts, and slid my suit straps over my shoulders, slowly exposing my breasts.

His eyes devoured me, making me squirm as he pulled my suit down over my belly. I lifted my hips for him, letting him peel it off the rest of the way, laying there and just letting him look at me. His eyes lingered between my legs and he used his fingers to part my smooth lips, his look almost pained as he saw the pink flesh inside.

"Can I taste you?"

I nodded, letting my legs fall open, hearing him moan as he settled between my thighs and started kissing my pussy lips. He took his time, slow, gentle, hesitant even as his lips brushed over my clit. He explored gently with his fingers, pressing first one inside of me and then two, making me rock my hips and whimper.

"Lick it," I whispered, reaching down and spreading my lips open. His breath was hot, his eyes dark with lust. "Here..." I showed him with my finger, rubbing my clit back and forth. He leaned in and touched my clit with his tongue, making me moan in response. Clearly encouraged by my response, he began to lick me eagerly, his fingers pressed deep inside.

"Finger me, too," I begged, rocking my hips. He did as I asked, plunging his fingers into my wetness and the pulling them out, doing it again, again, making me moan softly and thrust my hips. "Lick me," I whispered, reminding him, spreading my pussy wide and he groaned as he found my clit again with his tongue, licking me in short, flat strokes.

"You taste so good," he murmured, finally catching a good rhythm, licking and fingering me at the same time.

"You like the taste of pussy?" I asked, smiling as I half sat up on my elbows to watch him. He nodded eagerly, showing me rather than saying anything, sucking my clit greedily.

"Swallow all my juices, baby," I encouraged, grabbing a handful of his dark hair and pressing him against my pussy. I ground my mound against his face, making him moan. "Ohhhh god, yes, yes, make me come, make me come all over your face!"

I could barely hear him, his sounds so muffled by my flesh, but I don't think he cared. I bucked and writhed on the blanket, giving him every last bit of my orgasm, my whole pussy spasming, on fire, around his thrusting fingers. But they weren't enough. God, not anywhere near enough. I wanted his cock. I wanted it desperately.

"Come here," I urged, reaching for him, kissing his mouth, licking my juices off his lips, his chin. "God, I love that taste."

His eyes lit up when I said that, and he groaned when I yanked down his suit and grabbed his cock in my fist. I pushed him back on the blanket, nuzzling his cock as I settled myself between his legs. I was hungry for him, but I made myself wait, teasing his balls with my tongue, rubbing the head of his cock with my thumb.

"Oh god, please," he begged, looking down at me with half-closed eyes. "Suck it, Ronnie. Suck my dick."

I rubbed the tip over my lips, rolling my tongue slowly, wetly, around the head. He groaned, arching, toes curling, and I marveled how much he looked like Doc in that moment, and that less than twenty-four hours ago, his father's cock had been in my mouth, too. The thought was blackly exciting.

Of course, I knew better than to spend too long with his cock in my mouth. Not if I wanted to fuck him—and I did. My pussy was dripping and aching to be filled. I teased him for a few moments, then sucked him deep, all the way into my throat, and he marveled at it, lifting my hair out of the way so he could watch, his mouth half-open in astonished pleasure.

"I want your cock," I breathed as I moved up to straddle him.

"Inside you?" Henry's eyes went wide and I stopped, looking down at him, surprised. His cock was wet and throbbing in my hand, and I squeezed it gently, making him gasp.

"Haven't you ever...?" I smiled down at him as I teased my clit with the head of his cock, biting my lip, trying to hold myself back.

He swallowed, shaking his head, his hands moving to grip my hips.

"Do you want to?" I asked, aiming him, the tip of his cock poised at the entrance of my pussy.

"Yeah," he breathed, looking up at me, his palms moving up over my hips, my sides, cupping my breasts. "Yeah, put it in. Oh god, yeah. Please. Fuck me, Ronnie."

I never would have taken him for a virgin, but there was no turning back now anyway. I needed his cock. I had to feel him inside of me. I slowly shifted my hips, letting the wet heat of my pussy slide down his shaft. Henry gasped, his eyes widening, then closing, lost in the sensation.

"Feel good?" I smiled as he opened his eyes, staring at me in wonder.

"Better than anything," he agreed, already breathless, his hips moving up, experimenting, and he groaned. "You're so wet... god, it's sooo hot inside..."

"Nothing like your hand, is it?" I asked, teasing as I began to rock. He grabbed my hips, holding on, shaking his head.

"Oh god... so much fucking better..."

I knew he wouldn't last long, and I wanted to come with him. I wanted to see his face when he came inside a woman for the first time—when he came inside *me*. I moved his hands to my breasts, showing him how to squeeze and tug at my nipples. He took the initiative and grabbed my shoulders, pulling me close and sucking them, first one, then the other.

"Oh Henry," I moaned as his hips began to thrust, taking over the motion. I wasn't fucking him anymore, he was fucking me—hard and fast and furious, slamming his cock deep. I let him, reaching down to rub my clit, feeding him the hard wet tips of my nipples, riding him, barely keeping my balance. We were both working for it, breath coming fast.

"Can I come?" He groaned and bit his lip. "Oh fuck, can I come? Can I come inside you?"

"Yes, yes, yes," I said, rolling my hips on his cock, nudging my clit toward my own climax. "Do it, Henry, fill my pussy with your hot cum!"

He growled and thrust up hard, gasping and shuddering underneath me. I felt his cock exploding, throbbing, and I cried out and bit his shoulder as I came, too, my pussy quivering around his shaft, hot, wet, deep spasms that sucked him in deep with every sweet clutch.

"Oh god," he whispered, pulling me close, not letting me move off him. "No, don't. I want to stay inside you. I want to do it again."

I groaned softly, but I smiled, nuzzling his neck and shoulder, kissing the place where I'd bitten him and left a mark.

"Tell me something," I murmured, closing my eyes, feeling the heat of the sun against my back, his fingers making sweet, light shivery trails down my back.

"Hm?" His eyes were closed and he was smiling.

"Were you thinking about your sister when you were with me?"

"Are you kidding me?" He opened his eyes and laughed. "No way. Not for a minute."

I grinned and squeezed my pussy muscles tight, making him groan. "I didn't think so."

Chapter Nine

"Janie?"

I should have just turned around and walked away. That's what I told myself when I opened the bathroom door and found her sitting on the edge of the tub, tears streaming down her face. But I couldn't do it. I'd spent years wiping away her tears, and in spite of her new apparent loathing of me, I couldn't just turn those feelings off like flipping a switch.

"Go away," she said, sniffing and wiping at her tears, shaking her head as I came in and shut the door behind me.

"Is it Brian?" I sat next to her on the side of the marble tub, looking at her in the mirror, head down, long blonde hair hiding her face. "Sweetie, I am so sorry. I wish—"

"Henry told me." Janie shrugged, still not looking up. "He told me about how you saw Brian and Liz in the bathroom at Captain Tony's..."

I nodded, pursing my lips. "I'm really sorry."

"He was just someone to have fun with on vacation anyway." The tone of her voice told me that wasn't exactly true and the pain on her face emphasized it when she looked up and met my eyes in the mirror. "I don't care."

"Oh Janie." Instinctively, I slid my arm around her and pulled her to me. To my surprise, she didn't resist, resting her head on my shoulder with a shaky sigh. "I wish I could make it all go away..."

"Yeah, well I wish you hadn't gone away in the first place." Her words were angry and bitter and I winced. What could I say to that? I didn't have a chance to form a response, because she was talking about. "We used to have so much fun." She sighed, surprising me again by snuggling closer, reminding me of how we used to do this all the time. God, we had always been so close...

I nodded. "I loved babysitting you guys. You were...just like family."

- 115 -

"You were like the older sister I never had." She lifted her head to look at me. Her eyes were the same, just as blue and bright and beautiful. "I was just at that age, you know, right before puberty? I looked up to you. I wanted to be just like you."

I smiled, brushing her hair away from her eyes. "I'm actually glad you're not."

"I hated you for leaving." Janie looked away, shaking her head, her jaw tight. "For a long, long time." She was quiet for a few moments.

"And now?" I asked, hesitant to say anything really, to break the spell. I didn't want her to stop talking, to go back to being the angry Janie I didn't recognized.

She glanced sideways at me and frowned. "I guess I'm still a little mad."

"Well, you know…" I pulled her close again, taking her hand in mine. "After that vacation we spent here in Key West, your mom and dad decided to hire Gretchen as your nanny, and I…well, I had to go live my own life."

"But Ronnie, you never even called!" She met my eyes in the mirror and they flashed with anger. "You never answered my letters, you never even sent a stupid Christmas card! All those years, and all of a sudden, it was like, we didn't exist anymore to you…"

I felt tears stinging my eyes, and I realized, in my selfishness, what I'd done. She'd just been a kid. How was she supposed to understand the motivation of adults? She certainly couldn't have understood the shame and fear that had come up for me around the time I'd spent with her parents and with Gretchen. All she knew was that I'd left without even saying goodbye. I'd abandoned her. No wonder she was so angry with me.

"It was wrong." I turned and cupped her face in my hands like I used to when she was young and I wanted her full attention. "And I'm sorry. Really, really sorry."

"Why?" she whispered, her face bewildered, her eyes filling with tears, too. "I just want to know why."

Oh god. Why? I couldn't tell her that. I couldn't explain how that vacation had awakened things in me, parts of me I never knew existed, how being lovers with her parents had changed me, irrevocably, forever. How I'd wanted to run away from it—I knew that now, that I'd run away. I spent almost a year with Gretchen before I left her for some guy—any guy, no one special—because I was too afraid to admit I wanted more.

And TJ had known. Somehow he had known. That realization came to me in that moment and suddenly I couldn't breathe. He'd known my secret all along, that Doc was right—my capacity to love was too great to be bound by one. I had always wanted more, and I'd deprived myself, force-fed myself a diet of monogamy and in the meantime, wasted away...

"Was it because of what happened between you and my parents that summer?" Janie's question brought me out of my reverie, and I looked at her, trying to decide what to say.

"I really wish you guys hadn't found out about that..."

"Oh come on, even if we *hadn't* seen you with Mom and Dad..." Janie smiled, shaking her head. "I mean, Gretchen's been our 'nanny' for almost ten years. And we've been way too old for a 'nanny' for most of that."

She seemed so okay with it, but I wondered if she really was. She'd certainly used it to dig at me on more than one occasion over the past week, but Janie had always been good at finding and pushing my buttons. Maybe it was just her anger at me for abandoning her coming out.

"How do you feel about Gretchen...being with your mom and dad...?"

"I love Gretchen," she said simply. "And I love my mom and dad. I guess in some ways, their arrangement makes sense. I mean, at least if you're up front about it, you don't get hurt."

Out of the mouths of babes. Here I was, struggling with it all along, and she had a complete acceptance of the idea of polyamory that I had to come to through painful self-reflection.

"You mean cheating?" I asked. "Like what Brian did?"

"It's awful." Janie frowned. "It makes you feel so...betrayed. Violated."

I gave her shoulder a squeeze. "I'm sorry he treated you that way."

"I'm sorry I treated you the way I did." She gave me a small, apologetic smile. "I've been such a brat."

"Yeah, a little bit," I agreed, grinning.

"I just wish you'd been here." Janie sighed. "A part of our lives."

"You know what? I do, too. I didn't realize how much I missed you guys until I came back. I think I tried to block it out."

She looked down, frowning. "For a long time, I thought it was just because you didn't love us anymore."

"No," I reassured her. "The truth is, I didn't want to think about what I was missing, if that makes sense. I loved you *too* much."

She hugged me hard, and at that moment, I knew we were okay again. *It will all work itself out,* I thought. Trusting that had been hard, but here we were, hugging in the bathroom and back on good terms again.

"Will you do something for me?" Janie asked, letting me go and looking into my eyes, all serious now.

"Sure."

She swallowed and looked toward the sink. "Will you look at that test on the counter and tell me what it says? I'm too scared."

My jaw dropped and I saw a unmistakable white stick, the same brand I'd used myself when I was testing, I realized, sitting on the counter. "You're pregnant?"

"I don't know." Janie pursed her lips, blinking fast. "You tell me."

"Oh no. Janie..." I was already reaching for the test. She was so young, just barely drinking age for god's sake. What was she going to do if she was pregnant? I stared at the window, uncomprehending for a moment, unable to remember how to even read one of these things. "It's two lines if you are and one if you're not, right?"

Janie nodded, pointing at the counter. "The instructions are right there."

"If you are..." I picked up the directions, scanning through for the illustrations. "Is it...Brian's?"

"Couldn't be anyone else's." She pulled her knees up and resting her chin on them, looking at me. "I was a virgin until last week."

I gaped at her. "Brian was...your first?" That surprised me, given her age and her looks and...well, who was a virgin at twenty-one anymore? "Janie, you waited so long...why him? You'd only known him—"

"Two weeks," she agreed, looking at me, helpless. "I don't know. He was so sweet, and he told me he loved me. I just...gave in. I mean, I figured it was time..."

"Well," I said, handing her the test. "You're not pregnant."

"Oh thank god!" Janie looked from me to the test and back again.

"Or you tested too early," I countered, seeing her frown. "When are you due?"

"Five days ago."

I did the math in my head. "Well...the good news is, the test says you're not."

She looked up, hopeful. "Does that really mean I'm not?"

I shrugged. "Did you use birth control?"

"I'm on the pill," she replied. "I have been for years, my mom took me when I was fifteen. I had really irregular periods."

I could imagine Mrs. B doing that. She'd be more aware than most mothers of the dangers. "Then you know...it's probably stress. You've had enough stress the last week to last you a lifetime."

She sighed. "I really hope I'm not pregnant."

"Me too. You're a little young for that responsibility yet." I held my hand out for the test and she handed to me. "You'll have to test again if your period doesn't show up in a couple days, though."

"I will." She agreed, watching me shove the test and directions back into the box. "But I hope it shows up."

"Me, too."

Janie smiled at me, the relief showing on her face. "Is your husband coming soon?"

I nodded. "Tomorrow."

"Is he nice?"

"I think so." I smiled, looking forward to introducing TJ to the Baumgartners now.

"Is he cute?" she asked, perking up even more.

I laughed. "I think so."

"Do you have pictures?"

I nodded. "Sure. I have some in my wallet of him and my daughter, Beth."

"Can I see?"

I held up the pink and white pregnancy test box. "Uh, what do you want to do with this?"

She grabbed it and tucked it into the waistband of her jeans, pulling her top over it and fluffing it out. "Let's you and me go dispose of the evidence."

She took my hand and dragged me down the stairs. The Baumgartners and Gretchen were in the kitchen cooking dinner, and I heard Henry's voice too, as Janie and I sat on the couch and I pulled out my purse.

"Oh, Ronnie, she's so cute!" Janie squealed, looking at a picture of Beth. "She looks just like you."

I smiled fondly at the photo, feeling a stab of pain in my middle. I really missed my baby. Janie flipped to the next photo—a wedding one.

"Gorgeous," Janie murmured, touching the plastic covering the picture. Then she looked up at me and grinned. "And he's a hunk and a half!"

I laughed, and the sound drew attention in the kitchen.

"Everything okay out here?" Carrie stuck her blonde head around the corner, raising her eyebrows when she saw me sitting amicably with her daughter on the couch.

"Fine, Mom!" Janie replied, rolling her eyes and taking my hand. "Ronnie and I are going for a walk."

"Dinner's in fifteen minutes," Gretchen called, sticking her head out around Mrs. B's. "Don't make it a long one."

"We'll be right back!" I replied, shrugging and smiling at them both as Janie pulled me outside and shut the door wall behind us.

"They're so nosey," she said, making a face as we walked toward the water. It was the third time I'd taken this walk around the shoregrass, and recalling both prior memories made me feel warm all over.

"This is a good spot," Janie said finally, stopping behind the cabanas—I wasn't about to tell her it was the very same one her brother had masturbated behind while he watched her having sex—and pulled the pregnancy test out of her waistband.

"You won't tell my mom, will you?" she asked, sinking to her knees and digging a hole in the sand.

"Not if you don't want me to," I agreed, bending down to help her. If I was going to be a co-conspirator, I figured I might as well go all the way.

"She might freak out," Janie said, making a face as she shoved the test into the hole and started covering it back up.

I nodded. "She might."

"I didn't like being mad at you." She patted the sand down, looking satisfied.

I smiled. "I didn't like you being mad at me, either."

"Well come on," she said, brightening as she stood and took my hand. "Let's go catch up on everything."

"Ten years..." I smiled as we started to walk back to the house. "That's a big catch-up."

"That's okay," she said, swinging my hand. "We've still got time."

* * * *

"That was beyond bad." I yawned and stretched as Gretchen turned off the movie.

"Poor Nick Cage," Gretchen agreed, shaking her head. "Too bad he didn't 'Know' how bad that movie was gonna be before he accepted the job!"

"Ooooo bad pun," Carrie groaned beside me, snuggling closer to Doc. "I think we need to give up movies on vacation. We never get any good ones. Besides, we could be doing this at home."

"Yep," Doc agreed. "We should all be doing something we can't do anywhere else." His hand moved from his wife's shoulder over to mine and I flushed, but smiled.

"Oh I don't know." Gretchen put the DVD back into its rental case. "I remember having lots of fun with movies on vacation."

My eyes widened and I stared at her.

Carrie turned and grinned at me. "Is that so?"

"Uh..." I shook my head at Gretchen. She wouldn't dare, I thought.

"You remember, Ronnie." Gretchen put her hands on her hips. "What was the name of it? 'Doing the Babysitter' or something like that?"

"Gretchen!" I groaned, blushing, pressing my hands to my cheeks to cool them.

Doc chuckled. "That was a good one."

"This was the night we went out?" Carrie asked, raising her eyebrows.

I nodded, remembering, and cleared my throat. "That was...yeah...the first time..."

"She showed me your dildo, Carrie." Gretchen laughed when I hissed and she looked at me. "You know she still has it, right?"

"You do?" I looked over at Mrs. B, who was smiling softly.

"Yep." Her hand moved over mine, sliding past, to squeeze my thigh. "Wanna see?"

"Come on." Gretchen held out her hand to me, and I took it. I knew exactly where we were going, what we were about to do, and I didn't hesitate or even think twice. "I think it's bed time."

The four of us went upstairs, past Janie and Henry's rooms—Liz had come by earlier for dinner and to play Monopoly with us, and then they all went to a movie. Janie and Liz were becoming fast friends, and Liz and Henry...well, I had my hopes.

The Baumgartners bedroom door was open, and Gretchen pushed it wide. I stood in the doorway for a moment, remembering the night I'd been seduced by Mrs. B on the beach. We'd come up here, and had been joined at an opportune time by Doc. God, that night... I shivered, and Carrie wrapped her long, tanned arms around my waist.

"What do you remember?" she whispered, the feel of her breath making my nipples harden.

"Everything," I said, looking at Gretchen and squeezing her hand, remembering the night she and I had first touched and kissed each other on the Baumgartner's bed.

"Good memories?" Doc asked, moving in beside us both.

Smiling back at him, I said, "The best," and ran for the bed, hopping into it and jumping up and down. Gretchen laughed and joined me, holding both of my hands, and then Carrie did, too. We jumped on the bed like little kids, collapsing finally in a soft, entwined, breathless heap. Gretchen's head was resting on my thigh and she began to feather little kisses there. Carrie was facing me, her breath warm and sweet, and she traced her fingers over my bare arm, fingering the spaghetti strap on my top.

Doc had pulled up the wing back chair from the corner of the room and was sitting, watching us, grinning. "Don't let me stop the fun," he remarked, his hand moving over the bulge in his shorts, adjusting.

"Not a chance," his wife countered, leaning in to kiss me. Oh her mouth...so soft and familiar and sweet. I kissed her back, feeling Gretchen sliding the silky material of my shorts down, my panties coming off with them. Carrie's full breasts pressed against mine as we kissed, her hand moving over my back, squeezing my ass.

"Mmmm," Gretchen sighed happily as she parted my lips with her tongue, and I moaned into Carrie's mouth.

"Isn't she good?" Carrie asked, sliding my top down and dipping her head to take my nipple into her mouth. My soft moans were enough of a reply. Now they were both sucking and licking at me, Gretchen's tongue lapping at my clit and Carrie teasing my breasts. I glanced over at Doc for a moment and saw his cock out, his hand lazily stroking. He gave me a wink and I bit my lip, burying my hands in Carrie's hair.

"Let me lick you," I begged her, my hands roaming over her breasts, tugging at her top. She knelt up, pulling it off and tossing it aside, leaning in to let me bury my face against the softness of her breasts. She moaned and tugged at her own shorts, sliding them down, her panties quickly following, and then she was straddling my face.

"Oh yeah," I heard Doc whisper as I parted her pussy lips, first with my fingers, then with my tongue. Gretchen moaned and licked me faster as she watched, and I focused hard on Carrie's clit, determined to make her come hard, my belly clenching at the thought, aching to taste more of her juices.

"Oh me too!" Gretchen insisted, twisting herself around and putting her bottom in the air. She was totally nude. Carrie leaned forward eagerly, spreading Gretchen's ass from behind and licking up and down her slit. Gretchen's tongue never left my clit, though, her fingers sliding inside of me as she licked, licked, licked, making me moan and writhe against Carrie's wet pussy.

"Mmmmmm faster," Carrie begged, rocking her hips on my face, moving her clit over my tongue. "Oh yes, Ronnie, lick my pussy!"

I groaned as Gretchen sucked my clit in hard, bucking my hips up, arching upward, wanting more. Our soft, breathless cries filled the room and I sensed Doc behind me. His fingers moved over his wife's behind, teasing her asshole, and then he handed me the big, black dildo I remembered from so long ago.

"You might want this," he remarked, handing it to me with a wink. His cock was engorged, tight in his fist, and I stopped licked her for a moment to stretch my tongue out for it.

He chuckled, rubbing it over my lips. "Soon. Not yet."

I rubbed the dildo up and down Carrie's wet pussy, hearing her moan when I slid the hard head into the entrance.

"Oh yeah!" she breathed, arching back, taking more of it. "Fuck me! Yes, fuck me!"

I pressed the black cock in deeper, fucking her slowly at first, then faster as she rocked back for more, more, more. I tongued her pussy, too, burying my face in her wetness, finding it hard to focus with Gretchen's mouth fastened over my own mound.

"Ohhhhh!" Gretchen got there before any of us, her mouth coming off my clit as she came, her teeth and nails raking over my thighs. I heard the sweet sounds of Carrie licking and sucking at Gretchen's pussy, the soft, throaty noises she made as she swallowed her juices.

Then Doc was behind me, sliding the dildo out of his wife's pussy and replacing it with the stiff heat of his cock. Carrie moaned, glancing back at him, her eyes glazed with lust. I grabbed the black cock and sucked on it slowly, watching Doc fuck her, his hands gripping her hips, his balls slapping against her clit with every thrust.

Without a word, I handed the dildo down to Gretchen, who resumed the sweet activity she'd been so focused on moments before between my thighs—this time with a familiar black cock in her hand. She teased my clit with it and then slowly slid it inside of me, making me gasp and arch. Her mouth made me crazy, persistent, tenacious, pushing me closer and closer to the edge.

I slid my hand under Doc's balls and held them gently aside as I licked Carrie's clit, making her moan and spread even wider. She put her face down by my pussy, too, and then I couldn't tell whose mouth was where, who was licking my clit or fucking my pussy, but the sensation was beyond incredible and I gave into it, my nipples hard, my body strung taut.

"Ohhhh I'm coming!" I moaned, shuddering on the bed, under the pile of bodies, a sweet configuration of flesh writhing and slapping and bucking as I came. Doc pulled his cock out of Carrie's pussy then and pressed it deep into my throat, making me take it even as my orgasm rocked through me.

"Okay girls," Doc murmured, slapping first my cheeks, then his wife's ass, with his cock. "Line up."

I giggled, but we did, grinning at each other as we laid side by side on the bed, first Gretchen, then me, and finally Mrs. B. Doc went to his wife first, sliding his cock up and down her wet slit, teasing her clit.

"You like that?" he asked as she gasped and arched. I knew she had to be close after all the stimulation I'd been giving her. "You wanna come?"

"Ooooooooooh!" Carrie spread her legs wide for him. "Stop teasing!"

He grinned and slid his cock in deep, eliciting a deep sigh from her as they rocked. I rolled to my side to watch, licking at Carrie's nipple. Behind me, Gretchen slid her fingers between my legs, probing, making me shiver. Doc glanced over at us playing, his eyes half-closed and dark with lust as he fucked his wife.

"Oh god, oh baby, I'm gonna come!" Carrie's nails dug into his forearms as her orgasm overtook her. I sucked her nipple hard at that moment, making her squeal with pleasure, her hips matching Doc's heated thrusts.

"My turn?" I begged, seeing the head of Doc's cock seeping pre-cum as he slid it from Carrie's pussy. He chuckled, moving between my legs.

"You want that?" he asked, slapping my clit with his cock while his wife still lay beside me, gasping for breath, her chest heaving, her nipples hard from her climax.

"I think it's your turn," Doc decided with a grin, moving between Gretchen's legs instead. I groaned and watched as Gretchen opened her legs for him and moaned deeply when he slid his cock, still wet from Carrie's pussy, into her.

"Yesss," Gretchen murmured, reaching down to play with her clit as he fucked her. I couldn't help turning to kiss her. Behind me, Carrie snuggled close, her breasts pressed into my back, her hand moving down to rub at my aching pussy.

"Ohhhh Doc, don't stop!" Gretchen begged, her eyes closed tight, her hand a blur between her legs. He thrust deep, gritting his teeth as he watched the three of us playing. "Make me come! Make me come!"

He did. I felt her body beginning to tremble with her climax and I licked at her nipple as if it were her clit, making her eyes fly open in surprise and pleasure. She grabbed a handful of my hair, pressing my mouth to her breast, her hips bucking up to meet Doc's hot, slapping thrusts.

"Oh! Oh! Oh!" I loved her orgasms, the way they took her over like that and receded slowly, with little tremors. Doc eased his cock out of her, she groaned in disappointment, reaching for him.

"Nuh-uh," I teased, slapping her hand away—except I wasn't really teasing. *"My turn!"*

"Yes it is," Doc agreed, settling himself between my thighs. Both Carrie and Gretchen turned in toward me at once, each of them sucking on my nipples as Doc slipped the head up against the top of my cleft, teasing my clit.

"Put it in," I begged, reaching to spread it open for him. He looked down between my thighs, groaning when he saw me opening not just my outer lips, but my inner ones as well. "Fuck me, Doc. Do it."

He aimed himself and then shifted his weight, spreading my legs further with his thighs as he plunged in deep. I moaned, biting my lip and closing my eyes, savoring the sensation. I felt the press of two women, one on each side of me, both of them moaning softly as they licked and sucked at my breasts. Doc's cock twitched inside of me, and I knew what was coming, the hard pounding I was about to get, and my whole body tingled with anticipation.

"Look at me, Ronnie."

I opened my eyes to meet Doc's. They were dark with lust, but something more, too.

"You love this, don't you?" he asked, shifting his weight, pressing in deeper, and I moaned. "One isn't enough, is it?" He nodded toward Gretchen, then to his wife. They both half-smiled, but continued to coo and suck and nibble at my nipples, making my pussy clench and release, aching for more. "You want me, and her, and her…"

I bit my lip, thinking about denying it, but what was the point? The truth was the truth. I was insatiable. I did want him…and Gretchen…and Carrie. Hell, I even wanted Henry… and Janie. Oh god. I closed my eyes at the thought, knowing it was true and not wanting that thought, but Doc insisted again.

"Open your eyes."

I did, halfway this time, and he leaned over to kiss me, hard and deep. "Tell me. Tell me you love it."

"Yes," I breathed, squeezing my pussy around the length of his cock and making him groan. "Is that what you want? Yes. Fuck yes. I love it. I want all of you. All of it. All at once."

He gave a low growl and moved his hips back and then in deep again, driving me toward the headboard. I gasped and clutched at him as he fucked me. There was no fooling around anymore, no teasing. He was all cock in me, thrusting hard and fast, his face a twisted mask of pleasure.

Carrie's fingers found their way down to tease my clit when Doc knelt up between my thighs, grabbing my ankles and pushing my legs back so he could fuck me even deeper. I moaned and writhed and said things—I know I said things, but I couldn't remember what they were. I begged him to fuck me, to take me, to make me his... I remember that much. I begged Gretchen, I begged Carrie, I begged them all for release, and finally, finally it came in an aching flood, my whole body flushed with fire and centered sweetly on my throbbing clit.

"Ohhhh fuck!" Doc moaned as my pussy spasmed around his cock, my climax drawing out his in an instant. There was no controlling it, I could see it in his face, even in my own daze of pleasure.

Carrie acted fast, grabbing his cock in her hand and pulling it out of me. The first spray hit the exposed hood of my clit, a geyser of cum, a hot surprise, and I bucked at the sensation. The next streaked across my lower belly toward Gretchen and her eyes lit up as she followed it with her tongue. Carrie did the same, actually catching the next blast with her mouth and turning to Gretchen with the white stuff dribbling down her chin. Doc groaned as he watched them kiss, sharing his cum between them over my still quivering belly.

The two of them had clearly done this before, and I watched, too, half-smiling. When my belly and Doc's cock were glisteningly clean, both women came up to kiss me, too, sharing the taste of him. Doc sighed happily and settled on the other side of his wife, watching us snuggle together in the big bed. I closed my eyes and turned in Carrie's arms, resting my cheek against her breast. Gretchen spooned me from behind, and I think we slept that way, although I don't know for how long before we woke to do it again.

It was a long, sweet night, and I savored every moment we spent forgetting about the morning.

Chapter Ten

"It's like he's always been part of the family." Gretchen sat down next to me on the blanket and I squealed when she gave her head a shake, spraying me with water. But I opened my eyes and glanced over at TJ and Doc, who were standing at the barbeque grill, each with a pair of tongs and a spatula, turning hamburgers and hot dogs.

"TJ's so extroverted," I explained, smiling and waving when he looked my way. "He gets along with everyone."

"I think Janie has a little crush." Carrie sat down on my left side, and I found myself remembering the other night, being sandwiched between them on the Baumgartner's bed, Doc kneeling up between my thighs...

"I don't think TJ minds," I said with a laugh, watching as Janie stole his Detroit Tigers baseball cap for the third time in an hour, just so he would chase her down the beach. Janie got a good head start this time but by the time they disappeared around the field of shore grass, TJ had almost caught up.

Carrie smiled, shading her eyes as she watched Henry and Liz playing in the surf. "Doc never minded the young girls having a crush on him, either."

Gretchen and I exchanged grins. God knows we'd both had huge crushes on Doc back then. It seemed strange to realize that Janie's little infatuation with TJ was quite similar to my own attraction to Doc when I was all of nineteen. There was something about an older guy, when you were that age, something fascinating, intriguing...and as a young woman, you just wanted to push the limits. You found yourself wanting to test the theory...just how attractive were you to the opposite sex?

I heard Janie squeal with laughter and saw TJ carrying her over his shoulder, kicking and screaming, toward the water. His intention was clearly to throw her in, but she hung on fast and he went down with her.

"You guys hungry?" Doc called, flipping another burger. My stomach growled in response. "Be ready in about ten minutes."

"I want a quick shower before we eat," I said, standing and stretching. I'd given in to Carrie's urging to borrow a bikini and get some more sun, and my whole body was slathered with oil, thanks to Gretchen. "I'll be right back."

Upstairs, I let the water run hot over my shoulders, soaping the oil off my body in warm, sudsy sheets. The steam was so thick I didn't see TJ until he opened the shower door and stepped inside.

"Hey!" I gasped when he grabbed me and pressed me back against the wall, his tongue forcing my mouth open, his cock already hard against my hip. There was no time to protest—he had my thighs spread and his cock aimed before I could say another word.

"Oh god," I whispered as he lifted me, gripping my ass and squeezing as he drove in deep, pinning me against the wall. "TJ... ohhhh god..."

He growled as he fucked me, short fast grunts to match his pace, and I hung onto him, wrapping my arms around his neck, my legs around his waist, letting him take me. His cock was like heated steel inside of me, and I took his length again and again.

"Come here," he said, and I groaned when he slid out of me, positioning himself on the shower floor. There was just enough room for him to lay, his knees bent, and he pulled me down into my lap. "Fuck me, Ronnie. I want your pussy so bad I can't see straight."

"What's got you so worked up?" Smiling, I grabbed his cock—so hard!—and straddled him, not even bothering with a little clit tease before I settled myself down into his lap, impaling myself on his length. He grabbed my hips and thrust up, groaning as I squeezed my muscles around him, rocking back and forth, up and down.

"Oh yeah," he moaned, eyes closed, biting his lip, and I don't know what it was—maybe an intuition, maybe the far away look of pleasure on his face—but suddenly I knew exactly just what had him all worked up. And instead of my prior reaction—which would probably have been a jealous fit—this time, the thought had me breathless and turned on in an instant.

"Are you thinking about Janie's sweet little pussy, baby?" I murmured, flicking his nipples with my thumbs. His eyes flew open and he gaped at me as I sat up on top of him, the water a cascade around us. "You are, aren't you? Wondering if her little blonde pussy is shaved smooth? Wondering how she tastes? How it would feel to slide your cock into that tight little hole?"

He groaned, closing his eyes again, shaking his head, but I knew it was true. I just knew it. I pressed on, still riding him, deeper and harder now, coaxing his cock toward an inevitably sweet release. "She's practically a virgin, you know. Imagine how tight and wet she'd be…"

"Oh fuck," he moaned, gripping my hips. "God, baby, I can't stand it, she's such a little tease…"

I grinned. "I bet she is."

"She's all over me," he gasped, looking up into my eyes. "And I don't think any of it's accidental."

I didn't think so either. The thought of Janie coming on to him, "accidentally" brushing up against him, touching him places she shouldn't…oh god. That thought made me tremble with lust.

"Would you like to fuck her?" I murmured, leaning over him, my hands flat against the wet tile floor, my nipples dripping water into his mouth as he sucked at them.

"God, yeah," he admitted, wrapping his arms around my waist, shoving me down and thrusting up hard.

"I'd love to watch you," I said, making him groan at the thought. "Want me to get her up on her hands and knees? Lick her little clit while you fuck her from behind?"

"Mmmmm yeah!" His cock throbbed as he pressed deep inside me, and I rolled my hips, imagining Janie between us like that and the sweet sounds of her pleasure. What would she taste like, I wondered. That thought made my mouth water. "God, I'd love to watch you lick each other," TJ gasped, thrusting deeper, making me tremble with longing.

"I'd love to taste her," I agreed, the sweet throb between my thighs too much to resist, imagining Janie, oh god, yes, I was, I really was, imagining her tongue lapping at my clit. I rubbed myself off, sitting up fully on TJ now, letting him fuck me, knowing he was imagining her, too.

"I want you to come all over her pussy, baby," I murmured, my head going back into the spray of the shower, wetting us both. "I want to taste your cum all over her cunt."

That was it—the image that pushed us both over the edge, the thought of TJ exploding a white-hot shower of come over Janie's nearly-virgin pussy. I shuddered and ground my hips against him as my climax took me in an instant, sending me soaring over a sweetly perilous edge of pleasure. TJ grabbed my hips, unable to resist my orgasm, and I knew he was picturing it as he came up inside of me—he wasn't filling my pussy, but aiming each hot burst of cum toward the waiting pink of Janie's cunt, watching it drip toward my waiting mouth...

"Oh god," I murmured, using my hands against the wet tile to steady myself. "Oh my god... that was..."

"I'm sorry," TJ murmured, sitting up and hanging onto me. "Were you...are you okay? I didn't mean..."

"Oh baby, you have no idea." I laughed, wrapping my arms around him. "It's your fault, you know. You made me come here. You encouraged me."

He pushed wet strands of hair out of my face, his eyes searching. "You mean...you're not mad? Or...jealous? Or...something?"

"No." I grinned. "I'm turned on as hell...and wondering how we can get Janie into our bed."

TJ swallowed, his eyes bright. "There's a thought."

"I'm afraid you created a monster," I said with another laugh as I hugged him close, his cock still half-hard inside of me.

A knock on the door made us both jump, and I wasn't surprised at all that it was Janie, saying, "You guys? Dad says dinner's getting cold!"

"We're coming!" I called, grinning at TJ. Coming, indeed.

* * * *

"Where's TJ?" Janie asked, glancing up as I came down the stairs.

"I tucked him into bed in Gretchen's room.." I smiled, sitting on the couch beside her where she was typing away on her laptop. "Jetlag. He's exhausted."

"Where did Henry and Liz go?"

Janie waved her hand toward the door. "Out somewhere. I don't know what he's gonna do when we have to leave."

"Vacation romance," I agreed, grabbing the remote and flipping through the channels. Glancing over at Janie, I asked, "And what about yours? You still upset about Brian?"

She shook her head, making a face. "I just wish I could, you know, squeeze his balls in a vice or something for a few hours."

I laughed. "Now there's an image."

"Although I have to admit…" Janie bit her lip, pausing in her typing and staring at the screen.

"What?" I prompted.

"I kind of miss…" She looked sideways at me and half-smiled. "You know…fooling around."

"Oh that." I smiled back. "Well he was your first."

"But Ronnie," she sighed, sounding almost whiny. "I miss it *so much.*"

I nodded sympathetically. "What part do you miss most?"

"Well...I do miss..." She flushed. "Having him inside of me. Did you miss TJ? The first week you were here, I mean...?"

"Yes." I wasn't about to tell her I'd alleviated that ache with her father...*and* her brother. "What else do you miss?"

"I also miss..." She swallowed, looking down. "His mouth..."

"He was a good kisser?" I misunderstood her meaning purposefully, watching her squirm. God, she was beautiful.

"No...well, yes..." She laughed, shaking her head. "But I mean... down there."

"Ohhhh." I smiled, nodding. "Yeah, that's...mmm. God, yeah, I'd miss that, too."

"But I've been doing *that* a lot longer." Janie looked at me, her eyes bright.

"Is that so?"

"All the girls do it together now," she said, meeting my eyes. Her look was both defiant and inviting. It made my knees weak. "Honestly, it feels so good, it's hard not to..."

"So you've been with girls before?" I asked. She nodded, her eyes never leaving mine. "Did you like it?" She nodded again, slowly, licking her lips. Such a pretty mouth. My belly clenched and I asked, "What did you like about it?"

"Girls are so soft," she murmured. "I love the feel of them...and ohhhh, the taste..."

"You like the taste of pussy?" I asked boldly, my voice low, feeling my nipples tingle.

"Yeah, I do." She nodded, not blinking. It felt like we were having some sort of sexual stare-down contest. "A lot."

"Well..." I broke first, looking away, flipping channels again and trying to hide my flush. "So, what are you doing there on your laptop anyway?"

"Writing," she replied, still not looking away from me. I swore I could actually feel her gaze.

"Writing what?" I flipped past the Food Network—too sensual—stopping at CNN. Something dry and boring. That was good. "A paper for school?"

"No. It's...well..." She flushed then, finally looking back at the computer screen. "It's...a story."

"A story?" I raised my eyebrows, curiosity piqued. "Like, a fiction sort of story?"

She nodded, biting her lip, saying quickly, as if she had to blurt it out or might not say it at all: "It's erotic."

"Really?" I cocked my head and smiled, really curious now. "Want to read it to me?"

She brightened. "You want to hear it?"

"Yeah," I said, although I didn't expect it to be any good. Erotica was no easy task, even in the hands of the best authors, but I was curious about what she found erotic. That part I was very curious about.

Janie cleared her throat and began:

"Oh baby, now this is the perfect instruction in self esteem." I rolled off his hot, sweaty body to my side of the bed. "Lesson number one—learning to love having recreational sex."

"Is that so?" He kissed my shoulder as I curled up and pulled the sheet over my hip. "What's lesson two?"

"Do you realize, we'd still be at dinner?" I snuggled back, feeling his cock twitch against my ass. Nice.

"I'm glad you cooked." His mouth. It was sweet and warm and wet against my back. I liked that.

I rolled toward him, twining my fingers behind his neck. "I'm glad we fucked."

"Where's David?" he asked, his eyes dark.

"David?" Okay, sometimes I liked playing dumb.

"You know, the esteemed lawyer slash husband to Michelle that lives here with you and makes it harder for me to find time to fuck you?"

Oh that David. "Los Angeles." David was in Los Angeles. David was mad at me. And that had nothing to do with what I was doing here in bed with Harry. Nothing at all.

I stopped her. I had to. "Janie, this is good."

She flushed, smiling. "You think so?"

"No," I shook my head, frowning. "I mean, it's *really* good. Like...*really.*" I was too surprised to be more descriptive or eloquent. "Go on. Don't stop."

She didn't. And as she went on, I found that the story wasn't just good...it was *hot*. She wasn't kidding when she said erotic. By the time she reached the end, I was breathless and squirming on the sofa, my crotch aching. But it wasn't just the sex—it was the story. It was fantastic - timing, pace, character - with the perfect ending. Just perfect.

"I found a new thai place—David, are you listening to me?"

"Of course I am." He was. He always was, even when I thought he wasn't.

"I ordered pad thai and the guy behind the counter said I was a hottie. Am I? Am I a hottie?"

"Yes."

"David, tell me the story." I nudged him with my elbow, distracting him from his paper. He closed it and smiled.

"Berkley. 2005. You were in the back row of Elliot's class, and I could tell you were bored and too smart for him. You asked the best questions of anyone. And I said to myself, 'I'm going to marry her.'"

"And you did."

"Yes." David kissed me softly. *"I did."*

"My god, Janie, that's..." I swallowed, trying to find words. "That was just amazing. I can't even tell you. I'm...speechless." I really was.

"Did you really like it?" She closed her laptop and set it aside, her eyes bright. "Did it... did it make you wet?"

I nodded. No sense in denying that. "Incredibly."

Crawling across the sofa, she put her head in my lap like she used to do when she was little, looking up at me with those blue, blue eyed. "Can I... feel?"

"Janie!" I sounded surprised, but I wasn't. I didn't think she could surprise me anymore. Her hand moved up my thigh, smooth, under the edge of my shorts. My panties were soaked, just soaked, from listening to her story, and her fingers played over the crotch.

"Can I...taste?" she murmured, turning her face into my belly, kissing her way down.

"Oh god."

"Please?" she whispered, her fingers moving under the edge of my panties,

"Oh god," I whispered again as she eased my shorts and panties down over my hips, and I let her, I did—I even helped. She didn't waste any time, and her tongue was practiced and sure, focusing instantly on my clit, making me moan loudly. So much for teaching Janie, I thought, spreading wider as her mouth fastened over my mound and her eyes met mine. She might be able to teach me a thing or two.

Her tongue was sweet heaven, and I gently rubbed my nipples as she licked me, her tongue making fast circles, her fingers exploring my wet cleft. Her long blonde hair tickled my thighs and I pulled it out of the way as I watched her, our eyes locked, my breath coming faster and faster. Her story had me aroused beyond belief—and know that she'd written it, that the words and images had come from her own imagination—made it even more exciting.

"You like the taste of pussy, don't you?" I asked, reaching down to spread my lips wider for her tongue, groaning when she moved her mouth back and forth with a fevered passion. Her enthusiasm was answer enough, and I ached to taste her, too. "Let me taste you, too, baby. Come here."

Janie stood between my thighs, pulling her t-shirt off over her head. She was still wearing a bikini top underneath, and she untied that at the top, turning around to let me undo the back. Her breasts were full, gorgeous, as she turned back to me, lifting and then letting them fall as I watched. She reminded me so much of her mother—a younger Mrs. B. God, that thought was exciting, too.

I rubbed my clit as I watched her pull her shorts and bikini bottoms off, groaning when I saw that she was shaved except for a tuft of blonde hair at the top of her cleft. I wanted to bury my face there, and I couldn't wait a second longer. I sat up, grabbing her hips and pulling her to me, making her gasp and then moan as I slid my tongue through her slippery slit. She responded immediately, trying to spread wider for me, and when that didn't work, she climbed up onto the sofa and stood, straddling my face as I licked her.

My crotch was on fire and I rubbed myself, thinking of her tongue, but too attached to her sweet little pussy, literally and figuratively, to change positions. Besides, looking up and seeing her tugging at her nipples, her blonde hair a curtain around her face, her eyes closed, her lip pulled tight between her teeth—that sight alone was almost enough to send me over the edge.

"Oh Ronnie," she whispered, rolling her hips now, moving her clit in circles against my clit. "Oh god, yes, yes, lick me, lick me good!"

I did, I did, my tongue lashing at her pussy again and again. Janie moaned and bucked, her hips rocking faster, her hands in my hair now, pulling me in. I could barely breathe and didn't care, feeling her thighs trembling, knowing she was close, so very close...

"Ohhhhh yes!" she gasped, arching. "Now! Coming! Ohhhh!"

I didn't let up, shoving my whole face against her mound, lapping up her sweetness—oh my god, she was so sweet, her flesh hot and wet against my cheeks and mouth and tongue. I licked at her quivering cunt until her knees buckled and she collapsed in my lap, her mouth finding mine, sucking at my tongue, making me groan as she tasted her juices in my mouth.

Her hips made little circles as she sat in my lap and I wished for a moment that I had a cock to shove up inside of her. What would it feel like, I wondered, that tight little pussy? Instead I probed her with my fingers, working them in, feeling her rock in response as we kissed.

"Your turn," she murmured, starting to slide out of my lap, but I grabbed her hips, shaking my head.

"Both of us," I said, leaning back on the sofa and spreading my legs. She laughed happily, turning around and positioning herself so her pussy was over my mouth, and her tongue—oh sweet god, her tongue—probed into my wetness. I found myself in the very position TJ and I had been imagining in the shower, except TJ was sleeping upstairs instead of fucking Janie from behind. But Janie and I...well, were following our decidedly naughty pursuits on the living room couch. And if anyone walked in...and they could, at any moment...

"Don't stop," Janie said, pressing her pussy down against my mouth. "I can come again... I can come a lot."

Oh. God. I sucked her clit between my lips, flicking it with my tongue, swallowing the sweet taste of her juices. I couldn't believe I was doing this, that this was the same Janie I'd babysat for years now straddling my face, her pink flesh exposed to me as her tongue moved in circles against my clit, sending sweet shivers through me.

"Finger me," she begged, arching back, her fingers sliding into me, too. I did as she asked, her wetness making it easier, but god, she was tight. I worked one finger in, then another, making her moan when I twisted them inside and started fucking her.

"Ohhhh god," she whispered, fucking me back, making it hard to keep my mouth fastened on her pussy, but I managed somehow. "Yes! Yes! Fuck me! Oh god I wish it was a big fat cock!" I groaned, because I'd been thinking of TJ, imagining his cock sliding just where my fingers were, his balls slapping her clit as I licked and licked her. "Don't stop! Oh yeahyeahyeah, make me come all over your face!"

I couldn't stop her—or myself—if I tried. She came in a hot, quivering flood, my whole face bathed in her wetness, and I lapped it up, my own climax following within seconds as she moaned against my clit. Her whole mouth covered my mound, her tongue working my clit furiously as she came, and I gave her my orgasm, thrusting my hips, bucking up and offering my wet, spasming pussy to her.

When she went to move, I grabbed her hips, kissing her pussy and thighs, making soft, happy noises, and she giggled as she turned around and lay on top of me, tucking her head under my chin. We laid there for a while, and I knew we should get up and get dressed—truly anyone could walk in; Henry and Liz; the Baumgartners and Gretchen; or TJ could wander downstairs—but I didn't want to move. Feeling her weight on me, the softness of her breasts pressed against mine, the velvet press of her thighs, it was all just too good.

"Are you okay?" I asked finally, stroking her hair.

She lifted her head, looking at me, her eyes bright. "More than okay."

I smiled, snuggling her closer and pulling a blanket down from the back of the couch to cover us. She was still quivering.

"Janie, I have to tell you something."

"Hm?" Her voice sounded far away and happy.

"You are truly an amazing writer."

She was quiet for a moment, but I could almost feel her swelling with pride. "Do you really think so?"

I nodded. "Yes. What are you majoring in again?"

"Accounting."

I laughed. I couldn't help it. "Whose idea was that?"

Janie made a face. "My dad's."

"I think you should be majoring in creative writing."

"I wanted to, but..." She shrugged.

"But?"

"It doesn't exactly pay the bills."

"Honestly...I think you're good enough right now." I smiled at her incredulous look. "What you need is an agent. Do you have anything else you've written?"

She nodded. "Lots."

"What's lots?"

"Four novels. Probably hundred of short stories."

"Are you serious?" I gave a low whistle. "Are they all erotic?"

"No." She smiled.

"But they're all as good as that story was, aren't they?" I asked.

"I don't know..." She flushed. "I guess so."

"Amazing." I took a deep breath, thinking about her future, stretching out before her. So much potential, so many possibilities.

"I could sleep here," she murmured, snuggling in closer.

"Why don't we?" I suggested, kissing her forehead. "TJ's crashed upstairs. Help me pull out the sofa bed."

We got the couch bed pulled out and were back in it within minutes, wearing just our t-shirts now. I pulled the comforter over us as Janie turned in my arms, spooning, her back to my front. She was already drifting off to sleep. I kissed her cheek, remembering her as a little girl but experiencing her now as a woman. The juxtaposition was surreal, and I closed my eyes, listening to the soft sound of her breath, the only sound in the room. I couldn't sleep for a long time, thinking about Janie, about what had happened, about the past...and the future.

I couldn't quiet down until I'd worked it out—but when I finally had an idea, and decided I'd talk to the Baumgartners about it first thing in the morning, my whole body finally relaxed against Janie's, and I joined her in sleep.

Chapter Eleven

I woke up sandwiched sweetly between Janie and Gretchen, the three of us spooning, Janie's back to my front and Gretchen behind me, her arm draped protectively over us both. I kissed the top of Janie's head and she smiled sleepily, her body slowly waking, tensing as she stretched, cat-like, in my arms.

"Know what I want?" she murmured, not opening her eyes.

"I can't possibly guess," I replied, feeling Gretchen waking, too, snuggling closer.

"Ronnie's special pancakes!" she exclaimed. "I haven't had them in years. Gretchen tried to make them after you left but…yuk!"

"You got it," I agreed, laughing at Gretchen grumbling behind me.

I was in no hurry to get out of our warm bed, though, with Janie's bottom perfectly shaped against my thighs, and I found myself considering the idea I was going to propose to the Baumgartners. I hadn't consulted Janie, or TJ for that matter—but Doc and Mrs. B were the place to start, I decided, sliding my hand over Janie's hip, feeling her wiggle and press back against me.

"Well…that's where you were all night. Good morning, ladies."

I glanced up to see TJ standing in the doorway, his hair tousled but his eyes bright as he looked at the three of us snuggled together on the sofa bed. I smiled up at him, seeing it in his eyes, that dark look of lust, and knew how much just finding us together like this turned him on. Proof of that fact tented his boxers almost immediately, and he turned, excusing himself to use the bathroom.

"You're so lucky," Janie murmured, her eyes closed again. "He's such a hottie."

I smiled. "He is, isn't he?"

"You damned well know he is." Gretchen squeezed my ass, making me squeak. "And I think you should share."

Janie turned in my arms, her eyes brightening. "Now *that's* a good idea!"

"Hungry girl." I kissed her nose and then, still smiling, crawled out of bed and headed toward the kitchen, calling: "Time for pancakes!"

When TJ joined us again, wearing jeans this time—something that would cover up his obvious arousal a little better, I noted with a smile—I was up to my elbows in flour, Gretchen was nursing her first cup of coffee, and Janie was sitting at the kitchen table, complaining about her growling stomach.

"How'd you sleep?" I asked TJ, mixing the pancake batter like I always did—by hand.

"Like the dead," he said with a snort. "I didn't even know where I was, or that you weren't in bed with me...until I got up." His eyes met mine and I smiled, knowing he was remembering just where he found me when he got out of bed. "Although now I *feel* like the living dead. I've got a kink in my neck you wouldn't believe." He rolled his neck with a groan.

"I'd give you a massage, but my hands are full," I said with a shrug, holding up my hands, still covered in flour.

"I'll do it." Janie smirked as she got up and slid in behind TJ's chair, her hands going to work on his neck and shoulders, making TJ groan even louder. "My brother says I give the best massages of anyone he knows."

I bet he does, I thought, moving around Gretchen to wash my hands. Thankfully, Henry's attention had been diverted from his sister lately to a certain spirited redhead. "Speaking of, Gretchen, will you go find out if Henry wants some of Ronnie's special pancakes?"

"My god, girl, your hands are incredible," TJ moaned, glancing over his shoulder at a beaming Janie.

Smiling and humming to myself, I began to pour batter onto the hot griddle, pretending I didn't notice the way Janie pressed her breasts against TJ's back as she massaged his shoulders. It wasn't long before the whole family was filling the kitchen, all clamoring for pancakes—even Doc and Carrie, who usually didn't care for the all-out sugar-fest that was Ronnie's Special Pancakes. I even made one for myself, not even calculating the serious amount of calories of the thing in my head before sitting next to TJ at the table and digging in.

"These are evil on a plate," Henry said, his mouth full.

"Poor man's crepes," I said with a laugh, taking another bite. They were just huge, thin pancakes, rolled up with applesauce and cinnamon sugar inside, topped with whipped cream and more cinnamon sugar.

"Oh my god, I can't even finish this," Carrie sat back with a laugh as Doc made a grab for her plate.

"I think I'll indulge," Doc said with a grin, starting in on hers.

"Okay, now we all need to go for a swim to work off the calories," Gretchen remarked from where she was putting her plate in the sink.

"Aren't you supposed to wait half an hour before going swimming?" I laughed.

"That's such an old wive's tale." Gretchen rolled her eyes. "So who's with me?"

"Me!" Janie jumped up from where she was sitting on the other side of TJ. She nudged him, "Coming?"

TJ nodded, swallowing a bite of his half-eaten pancake concoction. "Sure, in a minute."

Henry, Gretchen, Janie and Doc went upstairs to change into suits while Carrie started to clear the dishes.

"I'll get it," I told her. "I was the one who made the mess!"

She waved me away, smiling. "The cook needs to eat, too."

"Missed you last night," TJ murmured, sliding an arm around my waist and pulling me close.

"Missed you, too." I smiled, watching Carrie at the sink, washing dishes. "But no one wanted to wake you…"

His breath was warm against my ear, close. "I wish you had."

"Patience." I nudged him with my hip, glancing down at his now empty plate. "Are you going swimming?"

"Why not?" He picked up his plate, carrying it toward the sink. "What's the point of vacationing on the beach if you're not gonna swim, right?"

"Towels are in the linen closet upstairs," Carrie told him, taking his plate.

"You coming?" TJ asked on his way by.

"In a few minutes." I pointed to my half-eaten breakfast. "You go ahead." I winked at him. "Have fun." My message was unmistakable and I could have sworn he actually blushed as he turned, going to get his suit on. That made me smile.

Then it was just me and Mrs. B. She'd finished the dishes and poured herself a cup of coffee, joining me at the table.

"I like him," she said, sitting across from me and stirring a spoonful of Splenda into her cup. "He's good for you."

"Yeah." I laughed. "I kinda like him, too." I glanced across the table at her, knowing it was now or never. This was the best opportunity I was going to get. "Can I talk to you?"

She looked at me over the rim of her cup, her eyes unreadable. "Sure. What's up?"

I had no idea how to proceed, so I just said it, impulsively, the thing I was thinking, the thing I wanted. "Would you mind if Janie moved to New York with me and TJ?"

She blinked at me, setting her cup down slowly. "Say that again?"

I didn't. Instead, I tried to explain. "We're moving to New York at the end of this school year. TJ found a consulting job out there that will pay him double what he's making now, and I got a position in a private school," I said in a rush. "Only, I worried about what to do with Beth. We have no family out there, and I hate the thought of putting our daughter into daycare..."

"You want Janie to move to New York to be a nanny?" Carrie raised her eyebrows at me, taking another sip of her coffee.

"Not exactly." I cleared my throat. *Not exactly, indeed.* "I thought...well..." I changed direction. "Did you know Janie writes?"

"Sure." Carrie leaned back in her chair, looking at me. "She's written stories since she was little."

"Okay." I nodded. "But have you read anything she's written lately?"

"Not...well, I guess, not for a few years." She cocked her head at me, frowning. "Why?"

"Because she's good." I leaned forward in my chair. "She's *really* good, Carrie. And a girl with that kind of talent needs an agent. She needs a *New York* agent."

Carrie shook her blonde head, pursing her lips. "Publishing is such a long shot."

I nodded. "But TJ knows people. Lots of people," I told her. "That's how he got the job he did in the first place. He's got connections you wouldn't believe."

"What about school?" she asked, although I could tell she was more than considering it now. She looked cautiously hopeful.

"She'll graduate at the end of this year, won't she?" I smiled. "We're not moving until over the summer. She can come stay with us then." She didn't say anything, but I could see her thinking about it. "I was just thinking, it would be the perfect arrangement. She could provide childcare for our daughter in exchange for room and board...and she'd be in New York, where she could make connections, get an agent, even get published..."

Carrie put down her coffee cup. "Does she want this?"

Did she? I hadn't asked her. I hadn't even suggested it to her. But I knew. I just knew. "Yes."

"Let me talk to Doc about it, okay?" Carrie got up from the table, deep in thought. She put her cup in the sink and ran water in it, glancing at me. "I'll let you know."

I nodded, following her to the sink, putting my plate in. "Are you coming swimming?"

She slid her arm around my waist, pulling me close and kissing me tenderly on the mouth. I gasped at the press of her body, the sweetness of her lips. When she broke the kiss, she hugged me tight.

"I can't think of anyone I'd trust more with my daughter," she whispered, and then she was gone, heading upstairs to change. I stood there for a moment, stunned, thinking about the past, but more about the future and the potential it held for us all.

* * * *

"Who is that with Brian?" I asked Carrie as we stood at the bar, waiting for Captain Tony to mix us two fresh strawberry margaritas. She glanced in the direction I was looking and smiled, her eyes narrowing, cat-like.

"That's Lola!" Captain Tony had to practically yell to be heard over the music, and I turned my attention back to him as he set one of the margaritas on the counter. "She's my cousin!"

Captain Tony's cousin Lola was a tall, leggy blonde wearing a skin-tight leopard print dress and boots that came up to mid-thigh. She had herself draped nicely on Brian's arm and I bristled at the thought of him finding someone again so soon after his treatment of Janie and Liz. I looked at our table and saw them sitting together, their heads, one blonde, one red, bent close. Janie pointed to Brian—she'd obviously seem him—and laughed. I waved to TJ—he was sitting on the other side of Janie. Henry got up and pulled Liz out on the dance floor as I watched. Doc and Gretchen were already out there.

"Lola likes the pretty boys," Captain Tony said with a wink, putting another strawberry margarita on the bar next to the first.

"I'm sure he'll be very photogenic." Carrie laughed, picking up her drink and taking a sip. She winked back at Captain Tony. "I owe you one."

Captain Tony waved her comment away with a grin, turning to his next customer, but I looked at her, puzzled, as we moved back toward our table.

"What was that all about?" I asked as we threaded our way through the people. I looked for Brian and Lola at the bar, but they were gone, and a brief scan didn't turn them up.

Carrie took the chair Henry had vacated, and I took Liz's—they were dirty-dancing out on the floor under the old-style disco ball, the changing lights mirrored in their hungry eyes. Henry and I had passed in the hallway or smiled at each other over dinner a few times, but he hadn't been away from Liz much since they'd first hooked up, and I considered that a good thing, for both of them.

Carrie smiled cryptically. "You'll see."

"Come dance with me!" Janie grabbed TJ's hand and pulled him toward the dance floor. He shrugged helplessly at me, but I just grinned and waved him on.

"What are you up to?" I nudged her, sipping my margarita—god, it was strong! It made my eyes water.

"Me?" Carrie watched as TJ danced with her daughter. Janie was pressed closer than convention should allow, and she was whispering something in his ear. "What are *you* up to?"

I shrugged, flushing, wondering just what Janie was whispering to my husband. Two weeks ago, it would have made me crazy with jealousy. Now…now it just made me crazy with lust. Watching the two of them together made my ass clench and my nipples tingle.

"Did you talk to Doc?" I asked, my gaze shifting to them out on the dance floor. They were a sweet sight, Gretchen's head resting on Doc's shoulder.

"I did." Carrie nodded, taking a long, hard sip of her drink.

I hadn't expected to bring it up. I wanted to wait for her to tell me, but I was so anxious to know. I wanted to tell TJ. And Janie. I wanted it so bad I could taste it.

"If it's really what Janie wants..." Carrie slid a hand under the table and squeezed my thigh. "We're all for it."

"Really?" I gaped at her, my heart hammering in my chest. I'd hoped, of course, but hadn't really expected them to agree.

"She'll love it." Carrie looked at her daughter, turned in TJ's arms now, her bottom pressed to his crotch as she wiggled back against him. "We can't protect her forever."

The music suddenly stopped and the dance floor went dark. The whole bar objected in collective surprise and then the huge flat-screen TV monitors above the stage flickered on. There was no sound at first, just a picture, but I recognized both of the people on the screen—the woman was Captain Tony's cousin Lola, sitting up on a counter with her legs spread, her dress pushed up around her hips, and the guy fucking her was unmistakably Brian.

"Ah, here's the show..." Carrie sat back with a smile, crossing one long, tanned leg over the other. The whole bar was stopped now, transfixed, watching the scene on the screen. The sound piped in then through the overhead speakers, loud and clear.

"That's a good boy," Lola moaned, wrapping her thigh-high boots around Brian's waist. His jeans were down to his ankles, his bare ass clenching as he pumped his cock deep into her.

I gaped at the screen, looking over at a grinning Carrie. What in the hell was going on?"

"Do you like Lola's pussy?" the woman on the screen purred.

"Yeah...yeah..." Brian gasped, not slowing. "Feels good..."

The blonde reached down and lifted up the leopard-print dress pooled in her lap, revealing something that made me do a double take before she asked, "Maybe you'll like Lola's cock, too?"

Lola wrapped her hand around a not-inconsiderable length of flesh rising up from between her legs—and it didn't belong to Brian. He was still inside of her...him?... I stared in disbelief as the blonde began to pump his...her...cock, right up against Brian's stomach.

"Holy crap!" Brian tried to move back, his face a mask of horror in his realization, but Lola had him in a vice grip, her stiletto's digging into his ass as she pulled him in deep. "What the fuck?!"

"That's a good boy," Lola murmured again, her hand squeezing the length of her cock, pumping fast. "Fuck my pussy while I stroke my dick for you."

Brian groaned, not in a good way, and tried again to get away, but there was nowhere to go. Lola was a head taller than he was, and obviously a great deal stronger.

"You did this?" I leaned in to ask Carrie the question as she watched the scene, still grinning.

She didn't answer, but her grin widened as she raised her glass and said, "Go Lola!"

"Get off me!" Brian yelped as Lola wrestled him to the floor, the clear winner as she sank down onto his cock again, her own cock hard in her hand. "Jesus, you freak, get the hell off me!"

Funny how Brian's erection didn't disappear, though, I noticed, as the whole bar howled with laughter at his protest. Lola slapped his belly with her cock as he tried to buck her off by thrusting his hips.

"Oooooo that's good!" Lola squealed as Brian writhed and pushed at her. "You like Lola's pussy, don't you?"

Brian growled his protest again. "Get the fuck off me!"

"I'm going to get off," Lola said simply, quickly standing and planting a stiletto heel in the middle of his chest, lifting her dress high and pumping her cock fast. "All over you."

The whole bar cheered when Lola grunted and came, a fat splotch of cum landing first in Brian's gaping mouth, making him gag and turn his head as the next blast hit him in the cheek, the next threading across his chest and dripping onto the tip of Lola's black boot.

"You bitch!" Brian groaned and rolled away as Lola lifted her boot from his chest. The transvestite found her panties and put them back on as Brian gagged and crawled in the opposite direction.

"I'd keep that thing in your pants from now on if I were you." Lola smirked, grabbing her purse from the counter. "Or you might get an even bigger surprise next time." Lola looked right at the camera, blowing a kiss, and the whole bar erupted in laughter and cheers that only grew louder when the screen went blank and Lola stepped out from Captain Tony's back room.

"Thank you! Thank you!" The blonde fluffed her hair and preened. And I suppose we should have expected it—maybe they were, which was why Doc and Henry were right there, standing next to Lola as Brian lunged out of the back room to tackle the transvestite who had just humiliated him in front of a crowd of people.

"You aren't welcome here!" Captain Tony called as Doc and Henry disposed of a furious Brian out on the street. The bar was still buzzing about what had happened, but the lights were back on, as was the music, the disco ball lazily turning as if nothing had happened.

"What if he goes to the cops?" I asked Carrie, frowning as Doc and Henry came back in, both wearing identical grins.

"This is Key West." Carrie grinned. "A straight guy complaining he got seduced by a transvestite? Please. Tell them another sob story."

"What about the video?" I nodded toward the flat-screen monitors, dark now. "The witnesses?"

"This is *Key West,*" Carrie reminded me again with a wink. "A straight guy getting his comeuppance from a transvestite in Captain Tony's is the stuff of legend—no one's gonna be on Brian's side, I'm afraid. And all the evidence? Well…" She waved to Captain Tony, who winked and waved back. "That just disappeared."

"Well, you may not be able to protect her forever." I laughed, shaking my head and looking over to where Janie and Liz were leaning on each other, still laughing. "But you're sure going to try, aren't you?"

Carrie slanted a smile at me and then looked at Janie. "I'm her mother. It's the least I can do."

Chapter Twelve

I wanted to tell Janie about my idea—ask her what she thought—but I didn't get the chance before we finally got home, an hour after the bars closed. TJ and I just sprawled on the sofa bed after everyone else had gone upstairs. I'd had way too many margaritas and the room was spinning.

I did, however, have time to ask TJ.

"I thought we'd try it for a year," I urged past his momentary silence at the suggestion. "And it would be great not to have to worry about day care, and…"

"Oh come on, Ronnie." TJ grabbed me and pulled me close, making the already spinning room whirl even faster. "Just admit it. You want to take her to bed with us."

I blinked in the darkness at his directness, but that was TJ—he always managed to find a way to cut through the crap. Especially mine.

"Am I that obvious?"

Of course I was. He knew it. Carrie and Doc knew it too. *And they had still agreed.* I remembered Carrie kissing me in the kitchen, the hard hug and her words about trusting me with her daughter. She knew. Of course she knew—and that had been both her blessing and her goodbye to me, I realized.

A chapter of our lives, the vacation I'd once spent in Doc and Mrs. B's bed, had closed, and even if we'd tried to go back, it just wasn't possible. Life had gone on, the world had moved on. Gretchen was going to California, we were going to New York, Janie and Henry had grown up. We were splitting again in different directions.

TJ chuckled and kissed the top of my head. "I really did create a monster, didn't I?"

Maybe it was the alcohol talking, but I couldn't seem to stop the words. "I want this, TJ. I want it more than I've ever wanted anything. I want her, and I want you, too. I always knew I was this way…I always felt like I was missing something…"

"I know," he said simply, rocking me gently in the dark.

I felt tears stinging my eyes. "But now I can't...I can't go back. I can't close this door again. I don't... *I don't want to.*"

"You don't have to," he whispered, kissing my cheeks, finding tears there, and kissing me again.

"It's okay with you?" I asked, feeling a tightness in my chest beginning to loosen as I understood and realized his acceptance.

"Always has been," he murmured, settling me against him, tucking my head under his chin so I could hear his heart beating in his chest. "I'm just glad you're not pretending anymore."

I shook my head, laughing at myself. He'd known, had always known, and had pushed me exactly where I wanted to go all along. How foolish I'd been to worry, to think he would leave me or hate me or...

"I love you," I whispered in the darkness. "It doesn't change anything about how I feel. I'm your wife, and I love you."

"I love you, too, Ronnie." He hugged me closer still. "I told you before, I'm not going anywhere."

Now there was just one more person I had to talk to... Janie. When I thought of her, my whole body responded as if I were on fire and I knew, I just knew, she felt the same way. I'd seen the way she looked at and acted around TJ. She wanted it as much—if not more—than I did.

I thought for sure I wouldn't be able to sleep, but I'd had way more margaritas than I cared to admit and I drifted off in my husband's arms, floating away in a sea of sudden, unexpected happiness.

* * * *

"Janie?" I thought I was dreaming. She was kissing me awake, her naked body pressed against mine in the dark, her fingers seeking the heat between my thighs. "What are you doing?"

"Shhh." She kissed me quiet again, her mouth soft and supple, her tongue slippery, making me shiver. "He's sleeping."

Not for long, I thought, smiling as I spread my legs a little wider for her probing fingers, gasping as she found my clit with beautiful precision.

"I couldn't stop thinking about you," she whispered as she shifted her weight onto me. Her thigh parted mine and she lifted her fingers to her mouth, tasting me, making me groan. "You taste so good."

Next to us, TJ sighed and rolled to his back and we both stiffened, breath held, until he was quiet again, his breath becoming deeper, more even.

"I want to lick you." She was already pulling the covers off, sliding down between my legs, and I didn't protest as her tongue, sweet, soft, found the hard nub of my clit. I let my knees fall wide, closing my eyes and letting her take me, her mouth working against my pussy, her fingers slipping through the wet folds of my lips, searching for my hole. I shifted my hips, helping her find it in the dark, biting my lip to keep from moaning out loud when she slid two fingers deep into me.

I wasn't going to last long and I didn't want to. I wanted to come in her mouth, to give her my climax in hot, short, shuddering bursts, and Janie seemed determined to get just that. Her tongue flicked against my clit as she fingered me deeper, harder. I was afraid the motion would wake TJ, but he snored beside me, and I couldn't take the time to make sure he was really asleep, because my orgasm was coming, it was coming...

"Ohhhh!" I breathed, my hands moving through the mass of Janie's hair as my climax finally caught up me with, my whole body trembling as I came. She felt the tight spasm of my pussy around her fingers and made a soft noise in her throat, licking me even faster, making my hips buck up to meet her. I gave her every last bit of my come, pressing her mouth against my hot flesh, making her swallow my juices.

"Don't stop," I whispered, keeping her mouth there, a shuddering tease. "Oh Janie, make me come again."

She moaned and pressed my legs back with her hands, burying her face between my thighs, making me gasp out loud. Her tongue focused right on my clit, so sensitive, lashing at it, back and forth, and I cried out in pleasure as her hands roamed up by body and found my nipples, squeezing, tugging.

Lost in sensation, at first I thought the hand that fell over mine was hers, but then realized, as the finger and thumb encircled my wrist and pulled at my hand, that it was TJ's. He was awake, listening, and when he pulled my hand between his legs, squeezing it around the hard length of his cock, I knew he'd been slowly stroking himself, listening to us.

I knew she didn't know I had TJ's cock in my hand under the covers as I came in her mouth again, my clit throbbing against her flickering tongue, my whole body stiffening and then writhing with my orgasm.

"Janie," I gasped as she kissed her way over my thighs, my belly. I didn't want to let go of TJ's cock. Instead, I took her hand in mine, whispering, "I have something for you," as I led her slowly toward him.

"Ohhhh," she breathed as I wrapped her hand around him in the dark. "Oh god. Oh. Ronnie?"

"Come here," I encouraged her, sliding between TJ's legs, licking at her fingers now wrapped around his length. TJ moaned as I took the head of his cock between my lips, sucking gently. Janie felt her way, her fingers moving slowly up and down as I swallowed his length, down to where her hand wrapped around the base of his cock.

"Want to taste?" I asked, offering his cock to her. She didn't hesitate, taking him into her mouth, making TJ groan as she began to suck him. I watched her in the dimness, moving her hair away from her face so I could see him going into her mouth, watch the movement of his hips, his hand moving in her hair.

Leaning in, I kissed her over the tip of his cock, and Janie kissed me back, our tongue colliding over the fat head of his dick. TJ moaned and I felt his hand moving through my hair, too, pressing us both together as our mouths met over his member. Janie was eager for him and she nudged me out of the way to take his length again, gagging a little on his length.

I smiled, my hand on the back of her neck, pushing her down a little further, hearing her groan. "Do you like sucking cock?" I asked, knowing she couldn't possibly answer me. She moaned, though, gagging again as I held her there, feeding her his length.

"Such a good little cock sucker," I murmured, letting her come up, gasping, on his cock and cupping her face in my hands then, kissing her hard, her sweet little mouth sucking still, pulling my tongue into her mouth. "Let him taste," I whispered. "Kiss him, let him taste his cock in your mouth."

TJ let out a soft gasp as Janie took my direction, easily, crawling up him and finding his mouth with hers. He didn't make any sudden moves, letting her kiss him softly, slowly, and I let them explore each other. Her hand still moved between his legs, stroking his cock gently, and I stretched out beside him to watch.

"Isn't he a good kisser?" I murmured, sliding my hand down over Janie's bare back, cupping her ass, squeezing. I felt her spread her thighs in response, whimpering against TJ's mouth. Smiling, I slid my fingers down her crack, making her jump when I teased her little asshole, and then moving further into the slippery wetness of her slit.

"Oh yes," she whispered, turning her head toward me. I found her clit, rubbing it, making her moan loudly. "Ohhh god yes... right there..."

"You like that?" I reached down and grabbed TJ's cock, shifting Janie's thigh so she was straddling him, and rubbed her clit with the head of his dick. "How about that? You like that hard cock?"

"Ohhhh!" Janie arched, rolling her hips as I teased her clit. TJ wrapped his arm around me, groaning as I teased them both.

I pressed my mouth to TJ's ear, whispering, "Imagine how tight she is, baby..." I eased the head of his cock between her lips, not letting him fuck her, just rubbing him through her wetness. "Do you want that hot, tight little pussy?"

"Yes," he groaned as Janie leaned over him, offering her breasts, and he took them both in his hands, licking between them as if he couldn't decide which was better. She gasped and arched again as he focused on sucking one of her nipples, and she squealed when I leaned in and sucked on the other.

"Let's taste her," I whispered and TJ had her over on her back before Janie knew what was happening, both of us spreading her wide, our tongues warring against her clit, our fingers competing to get inside her little pussy. He managed to get one in, and I got one in, too, and we fucked her in unison, making her whimper and writhe.

"Ohhh please!" she begged, and TJ let me cover her mound with my mouth, my tongue focused, persistent, aching to feel her come. "Oh! God! Now! Oh fuck!"

I groaned against her cunt, sucking at it, hungry, greedy, eating her up, every last bit, as her climax rocked her whole body, her pussy spasming again and again around our fingers, the tight press of her hole clenching as we fingered her to orgasm.

"Fuck me," she moaned, reaching for both of us. "I want your cock. TJ, please. Fuck me."

"Me, first." I smiled, pressing TJ down onto the sofa bed and climbing him like a tree. He groaned as I slid my pussy down his length, rolling my hips at the base, using my fingers to tease my aching clit.

"Come here," TJ encouraged, pulling Janie toward him. She followed his lead, letting him position her, legs spread, pussy centered neatly over his face. Moaning softly, she leaned against me, and we kissed softly as I rode my husband's cock and she sat on his face at let him lick her.

"He's so hard," I whispered into her ear as we rocked, our breasts pressed together, our nipples kissing. "I'm going to let him fuck you."

"Please?" She groaned, wrapping her arms around my neck, hanging on. "Promise?"

"Oh yes," I reassured her, cupping her breasts in my hands, tweaking her nipples. "I promise. He's going to fuck you so hard, so good." She moaned into my mouth, grinding her hips down against his face. TJ groaned, too, a muffled, happy sound. "But I want you to come in his mouth, Janie. Come in his mouth while I come all over his big, hard fucking dick."

"Oh fuck!" She gasped, hanging tight, her whole body trembling against mine. I rubbed my clit faster, rolling my hips, feeling TJ's cock moving deep inside, and I was so close...so very close. "I'm gonna come for you! Yes! All over his face!"

She did, quivering and arching and begging us both for something, anything, and I came, too, my pussy squeezing TJ's cock again and again, making him moan and grab my hips. Janie moaned against my mouth as we kissed, our bodies slick already with a light sheen of sweat. I cupped her mound with my hand as she shifted forward, making her gasp.

"We're not done with your sweet little pussy," I reminded her, and she sighed happily as I rubbed my hand between her legs. "Get on your hands and knees."

She did, and I slid my body underneath hers, fitting our bodies together, exploring her still-throbbing pussy with my eager tongue. Janie bent her head in whimpering submission, rubbing her cheek against my thigh, my pussy, moaning softly as my tongue slid between her lips, looking for the sensitive bud of her clit. I wanted it again. Again.

"You like my fingers in you?" I murmured, sliding one in, fingering her slowly. She nodded against my thigh, putting her ass further up in the air. "You like it when I fuck you?" I began a slow rhythm, my fingers moving in and out. Beside me, TJ was on his knees, cock in hand, watching. The sight was almost enough to make me come again right then.

"Mmm god, Janie, you taste so good, baby," I whispered, swallowing her juices, literally scooping them out of her little hole with my tongue as I removed my fingers. She groaned when I did that and I smiled. "What's the matter? You wanna be fucked? You want something big and hard filling that tight little pussy?"

"Please?" She whimpered, nodding against my belly, her hands gripping my thighs. She begged and begged. "Oh god, please. Ronnie, please. Let him fuck me. I want it so much…"

"Shh." I rubbed at her clit with my fingers, making her tremble. "I know you do. It's okay. I'm gonna let him fuck you."

TJ moaned softly when I reached for his cock and he moved toward me on his knees, his head going back when I began to suck my juices off the tip. I cupped his balls in my hand, letting him feed me the length of his cock, opening my throat for him as Janie arched back, her pussy so wet and ready.

"You want that pussy?" I gasped, taking him out of my mouth and pressing him against the wet entrance of her cunt.

"Put me in," he begged, shifting his hips forward, and they both groaned as I finally let him slide into her, all the way in, his balls pressed tight against her pussy.

"Oh my god." TJ's hands gripped her ass and Janie ground her hips against him, making small, whimpering noises. "Oh baby, she's so *tight.*"

I smiled as he began to fuck her, taking short, slow strokes, and knew he was trying to last, fighting to hold on. Janie met him, begging for more, more. She gasped when my fingers found her little clit, rubbing it back and forth, teasing.

"Fuck her," I insisted, moaning when Janie's eager little mouth found my clit, sucking and licking, distracted by her own pleasure, but still... "TJ, do it! Fuck her hard!"

He groaned, pulling almost all the way out and plunging in deep. I sighed happily and Janie gave a low, guttural growl, her mouth covering my mound. Grabbing her ass, he drove in deep, hard, fast, long strokes now, bottoming out with each thrust. His balls slapping furiously against her clit and I rubbed it faster, making her beg for more.

"Oh TJ!" she whimpered, using her fingers to rub my clit as she gasped out the words. "I'm gonna come! I'm gonna come all over your cock!"

None of us could resist that. Janie came hard, bucking back against him, her body quivering with her release. My pussy spasmed uncontrollably as Janie's fingers made fast circles around my clit. And TJ—I grabbed him just in time, pulling him out as the first hot blast of his cum splattered the pink flesh of Janie's cunt. I jerked him fast and hard as he throbbed in my hand, his groans mingling with ours as he came, each thrust of his cock in my fist resulting in another hot spray of cum against Janie's pussy.

"Oh!" Janie squealed in surprise when I began to lick TJ's cum from her slit. I lapped up as much as I could and then sucked the head of his cock, too, for good measure, getting every last drop and making him shiver in response.

When we had Janie snuggled down under the blankets between us, all of us still a little breathless and dizzy, I remembered that I hadn't told her. I kissed the top of her head, stroking her hair and looking at TJ, smiling. .

"Janie...I have to tell you something."

"Hm?" She murmured, not opening her eyes but cuddling a little closer.

"We're moving to New York," I started, stroking her cheek.

"No!" Her eyes flew open. "You're leaving? Again?" She struggled to sit, but with TJ's leg over one of hers and mine over the other, it was an impossible feat. "You can't do this! No! You can't! I thought we would be together, that we would—"

"Shh!" I pressed my fingers to her lips, shaking my head. "Janie, shh!"

She quieted, but I saw the tears glistening in her eyes.

"Janie, listen..." I wiped the tears as they started falling down her cheeks. "We're moving to New York this summer, but we want you to come with us."

She was quiet for a moment and then repeated softly, "Come with you?"

I nodded. "New York is the best place in the world to be a writer." I felt her startle and smiled over her at my husband. "TJ will find you an agent. You can have lots of time to write. And the truth is, we need a nanny..."

TJ shook his head, leaning over and kissing her cheek, whispering into her ear, "The truth is, we want you."

Yes. That was the truth.

"We love you, Janie," I murmured, kissing another tear from her cheek. And that was the truth, too. "What do you think? Do you want to come live with us in New York?"

"Yes." Her tears had turned happy and she wrapped her arms around me, squeezing me tight. "Yes!"

I hugged her back, smiling at TJ, and his eyes said it all as he looked at us together.

"Oh nooo." Janie groaned, burying her face against my neck.

"What's the matter?" I tried to get her to look at me. "What is it?"

"Cramps." She made a face. "Damnit. I think I just got my period."

"Well that's a good thing," I said with a laugh. "That means you're not pregnant, thank god."

She sighed. "But that means we can't..." Looking hopefully between the two of us, she bit her lip. "Do this again?"

"This week, maybe, that's true." TJ chuckled.

"We'll have plenty of time together, Janie." I smiled and kissed her softly. "I promise. We're not going anywhere."

The End

ABOUT SELENA KITT

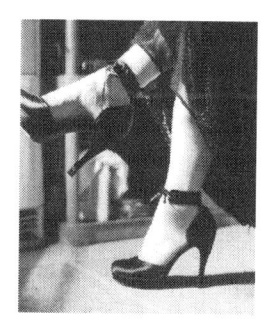

Like any feline, Selena Kitt loves the things that make her purr—and wants nothing more than to make others purr right along with her! Pleasure is her middle name, whether it's a short cat nap stretched out in the sun or a long kitty bath. She makes it a priority to explore all the delightful distractions she can find, and follow her vivid and often racy imagination wherever it wants to lead her.

Her writing embodies everything from the spicy to the scandalous, but watch out—this kitty also has sharp claws and her stories often include intriguing edges and twists that take readers to new, thought-provoking depths.

When she's not pawing away at her keyboard, Selena runs an innovative publishing company (www.excessica.com) and in her spare time, she worships her devoted husband, corrals four kids and a dozen chickens, all while growing an organic garden. She also loves bellydancing and photography.

Her e-publishing credits include: *Rosie's Promise* published by Samhain and *Torrid Teasers #49* published by Whiskey Creek Press featuring two short stories,

French Lessons and *I'll Be Your Superman* in 2008. Her stories and poems are in the following anthologies: *Coming Together: For The Cure, Coming Together: Under Fire* and *Coming Together Volume 1* and *Volume 3*. Two stories, *Sacred Spots* and *Happy Accident*, have been published by Phaze Publishing, as well as her novels *Christmas Stalking, Blind Date, The Surrender of Persephone. The Song of Orpheus* is coming soon! She has also been published online in <u>The Shadow Sacrament: a journal of sex and spirituality,</u> The Erotic Woman, her book EcoErotica, was a 2009 Eppie Finalist, and her story, *Connections*, was one of the runners-up for the <u>*2006 Rauxa Prize*</u>, given annually to an erotic short story of "exceptional literary quality," out of over 1,000 nominees, where awards are judged by a select jury and all entries are read "blind" (without author's name available.) She can be reached on her website at www.selenakitt.com

If you enjoyed <u>A BAUMGARTNER REUNION</u>, you might also enjoy:

BABYSITTING THE BAUMGARTNERS
By Selena Kitt

Ronnie—or as Mrs. Baumgartner insists on calling her, Veronica—has been babysitting for the Baumgartners since she was fifteen years old and has practically become another member of the family. Now a college freshman, Ronnie jumps at the chance to work on her tan in the Florida Keys with "Doc" and "Mrs. B" under the pretense of babysitting the kids. Ronnie isn't the only one with ulterior motives, though, and she discovers that the Baumgartners have wayward plans for their young babysitter. This wicked hot sun and sand coming of age story will seduce you as quickly as the Baumgartners seduce innocent Ronnie and leave everyone yearning for more!

Warning: This title contains MFF threesome, lesbian, and anal sex.

EXCERPT from BABYSITTING THE BAUMGARTNERS:

When my legs felt steady enough to hold me, I got out of the shower and dried off, wrapping myself in one of the big white bath sheets. My room was across the hall from the bathroom, and the Baumgartner's was the next room over. The kids' rooms were at the other end of the hallway.

As I made my way across the hall, I heard Mrs. B's voice from behind their door. "You want that tight little nineteen-year-old pussy, Doc?"

I stopped, my heart leaping, my breath caught. *Oh my God.* Were they talking about me? He said something, but it was low, and I couldn't quite make it out. Then she said, "Just wait until I wax it for you. It'll be soft and smooth as a baby."

Shocked, I reached down between my legs, cupping my pussy as if to protect it, standing there transfixed, listening. I stepped closer to their door, seeing it wasn't completely closed, still trying to hear what they were saying. There wasn't any noise, now.

"Oh God!" I heard him groan. "Suck it harder."

My eyes wide, I felt the pulse returning between my thighs, a slow, steady heat. Was she sucking his cock? I remembered what it looked like in his hand--even from a distance, I could tell it was big--much bigger than any of the boys I'd ever been with.

"Ahhhh fuck, Carrie!" He moaned. I bit my lip, hearing Mrs. B's first name felt so wrong, somehow. "Take it all, baby!"

All?! My jaw dropped as I tried to imagine, pressing my hand over my throbbing mound. Mrs. B said something, but I couldn't hear it, and as I leaned toward the door, I bumped it with the towel wrapped around my hair. My hand went to my mouth and I took an involuntary step back as the door edged open just a crack. I turned to go to my room, but I knew that they would hear the sound of my door.

"You want to fuck me, baby?" she purred. "God, I'm so wet ... did you see her sweet little tits?"

"Fuck, yeah," he murmured. "I wanted to come all over them."

Hearing his voice, I stepped back toward the door, peering through the crack. The bed was behind the door, at the opposite angle, but there was a large vanity table and mirror against the other wall, and I could see them reflected in it. Mrs. B was completely naked, kneeling over him. I saw her face, her breasts swinging as she took him into her mouth. His cock stood straight up in the air.

"She's got beautiful tits, doesn't she?" Mrs. B ran her tongue up and down the shaft.

"Yeah." His hand moved in her hair, pressing her down onto his cock. "I want to see her little pussy so bad. God, she's so beautiful."

"Do you want to see me eat it?" She moved up onto him, still stroking his cock. "Do you want to watch me lick that sweet, shaved cunt?"

I pressed a cool palm to my flushed cheek, but my other hand rubbed the towel between my legs as I watched. I'd never heard anyone say that word out loud and it both shocked and excited me.

"Oh God, yeah!" He grabbed her tits as they swayed over him. I saw her riding him, and knew he must be inside of her. "I want inside her tight little cunt."

I moved the towel aside and slipped my fingers between my lips.

He's talking about me!

The thought made my whole body tingle, and my pussy felt on fire. Already slick and wet from my orgasm in the shower, my fingers slid easily through my slit.

"I want to fuck her while she eats your pussy." He thrust up into her, his hands gripping her hips. Her breasts swayed as they rocked together. My eyes widened at the image he conjured, but Mrs. B moaned, moving faster on top of him.

"Yeah, baby!" She leaned over, her breasts dangling in his face. His hands went to them, his mouth sucking at her nipples, making her squeal and slam down against him even harder. "You want her on her hands and knees, her tight little ass in the air?"

He groaned, and I rubbed my clit even faster as he grabbed her and practically threw her off him onto the bed. She seemed to know what he wanted, because she got onto her hands and knees and he fucked her like that, from behind. The sound of them, flesh slapping against flesh, filled the room.

They were turned toward the mirror, but Mrs. B had her face buried in her arms, her ass lifted high in the air. Doc's eyes looked down between their legs, like he was watching himself slide in and out of her.

"Fuck!" Mrs. B's voice was muffled. "Oh fuck, Doc! Make me come!"

He grunted and drove into her harder. I watched her shudder and grab the covers in her fists. He didn't stop, though--his hands grabbed her hips and he worked himself into her over and over. I felt weak-kneed and full of heat, my fingers rubbing my aching clit in fast little circles. Mrs. B's orgasm had almost sent me right over the edge. I was very, very close.

"That tight nineteen-year-old cunt!" He shoved into her. "I want to taste her." He slammed into her again. "Fuck her." And again. "Make her come." And again. "Make her scream until she can't take anymore."

I leaned my forehead against the doorjamb for support, trying to control how fast my breath was coming, how fast my climax was coming, but I couldn't. I whimpered, watching him fuck her and knowing he was imagining me ... *me!*

"Come here." He pulled out and Mrs. B turned around like she knew what he wanted. "Swallow it."

He knelt up on the bed as she pumped and sucked at his cock. I saw the first spurt land against her cheek, a thick white strand of cum, and then she covered the head with her mouth and swallowed, making soft mewing noises in her throat. I came then, too, shuddering and shivering against the doorframe, biting my lip to keep from crying out.

When I opened my eyes and came to my senses, Mrs. B was still on her hands and knees, focused between his legs-- but Doc was looking right at me, his dark eyes on mine.

He saw me. For the second time today--he saw me.

My hand flew to my mouth and I stumbled back, fumbling for the doorknob behind me I knew was there. I finally found it, slipping into my room and shutting the door behind me. I leaned against it, my heart pounding, my pussy dripping, and wondered what I was going to do now.

BUY THIS AND MORE TITLES AT
www.eXcessica.com

eXcessica's BLOG

www.excessica.com/blog

eXcessica's YAHOO GROUP

groups.yahoo.com/group/eXcessica/

Check out both for updates about eXcessica books, as well as chances to win free E-Books!

And look for these other titles from Selena Kitt:

BLUEBEARD'S WIFE
By Selena Kitt

Tara's husband has never shared a fantasy with her, or even masturbated—that she knows of. However, this curious wife discovers a phone bill full of phone calls to sex lines and realizes her husband has been living a double life! Instead of getting mad, Tara's curiosity leads her to begin listening in on John's steamy conversations in hopes of finding out what he really wants in the bedroom. After several failed attempts at bringing fantasy to reality, however, a frustrated Tara turns to her much more adventurous best friend, Kelly, for help. A quick psychology 101 diagnosis from Dr. Kelly marks John as having a classic "madonna/whore" complex, and she quickly sets about making plans to rectify this situation. Tara goes along for the ride, hoping that Kelly may have the answer to bridging the seemingly ever-growing gap in her marriage...

Warning: This title contains a MFF threesome, a daddy/daughter role play between consenting adults, strong language, minor drug use and lesbian and anal sex.

NAUGHTY BITS
By Selena Kitt

David has been brightening up his gray Surrey, England days with the porn collection hidden in his parents' shed, but when he find that his older sister, Dawn has discovered his magazine collection, things really begin to heat up. Their parents insist that their just-graduated son look for a job, but their daughter has the week off and is determined to work on her tan. Distracted David finds himself increasingly tempted by his seductive older sister, who makes it very clear what she wants. Her teasing ways slowly break down the taboo barrier between brother and sister until they both give in to their lust... but what are they going to do about the feelings that have developed between them in the meantime...?

Warning: This title contains incest and anal sex.

ESCAPING FATE
By Selena Kitt

Sam has an unusual interest in humans—well, considering she's a fairy of fate whose profession it is to determine their futures, it's no wonder! But it isn't just Karma she's curious about... Sam has what her fairy-pal Alex thinks is an inordinate and rather wanton interest in certain biological aspects of human behavior—most notably, *s-e-x*.

When Sam's job leads her into the path of a handsome man who rocks her world, Sam's interest becomes obsession. Alex reminds her that fairies get one Christmas wish – will Sam consider using hers to become human to experience one night of bliss?

When things become even more complicated—Sam discovers that Drew, the sexy stranger she's been fantasizing about, can actually *see* her—Sam finds herself immersed in a complex and tangled web of human experience. She has to make a choice that will teach her a twisted lesson in fate, ultimately change the course of human existence and even reveal the origin of Santa Claus!

Warning: Contains graphic language and sex.

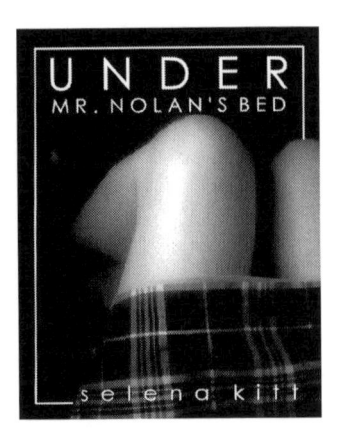

UNDER MR. NOLAN'S BED
By Selena Kitt

Leah and Erica have been best friends and have gone to the same Catholic school since just about forever. Leah spends so much time with the Nolans—just Erica and her handsome father, now, since Erica's mother died—that she's practically part of the family. When the girls find something naughty under Mr. Nolan's bed, their strict, repressive upbringing makes it all the more exciting as they begin their sexual experimentation. Leah's exploration presses deeper, and eventually she finds herself torn between her best friend and her best friend's father—but even she couldn't have predicted the shocking and bittersweet outcome of their affair.

Warning: This title contains a threesome, lesbian sex and incest.

THE SYBIAN CLUB
By Selena Kitt

Tasha convinces her husband, Max, to buy her a the ultimate female pleasure machine – a Sybian – but he only agrees if she can come up with a business plan to pay for it. Determined to keep her promise, she creates The Sybian Club and begins bringing women to the basement room set up just for her new toy. It becomes so popular, she has to enlist the help of new friend, Ashley, to keep up with the demand, and the women enjoy an exciting ride as the business thrives. But Tasha has developed feelings for Ashley, and doesn't know how to tell her husband that she wants to add more to their sex life than just a new toy...

Warning: This title contains a threesome, lesbian and anal sex.

TICKLED PINK
By Selena Kitt

Who says sex can't be fun - or funny? You'll find more than enough amusing mishaps and uproarious situations to tickle your funny bone–and more!–in this delightfully wicked and delightfully sexy anthology from Selena Kitt.

Warning: This title contains graphic language and sex.

TAKEN
By Selena Kitt

Lizzy's friendship with her older boss, Sarah, turns into something deeper and much more exciting one rainy day after work, and Lizzy finds herself drawn into a world she never knew existed. Sarah has a dominant streak, and as she leads Lizzy into the role of a submissive, the two women become closer than they ever thought possible. But while Sarah, hurt too many times, wears a ring, and tells guys she's "taken," Lizzy knows she secretly longs for a man. Determined to find one for them both to share, Lizzy is just about to give up when a dark, handsome, virile answer shows up right under her nose. Lizzy may think she and Sarah are going to seduce David—but she underestimates their handsome co-worker, and David turns the tables on them both. But will he be able to tame the untamable Sarah?

Warnings: This title contains graphic language and sex, a m/f/f threesome and mild bdsm elements.

BACK TO THE GARDEN
By Selena Kitt

Discover the deliciously taboo lure of an incestuous siren call with four stories bundled into a wickedly hot anthology that's determined to keep it all in the family!

Warning: This title contains graphic language, sex and mother-son, father-daughter incest.

ECOEROTICA
By Selena Kitt

2009 EPPIE AWARD FINALIST

Mother Earth is one hot, sexy Mama, and in this tribute to nature and the environment, Selena Kitt pays homage to her beauty, her grandeur — and her conservation. Who else could tackle topics like global warming, strip mining, animal endangerment and environmental toxicity, all while making it hot, hot, hot?

This anthology includes six sexy and environmentally provocative stories that will rock your world—and arouse and raise more than your environmental awareness. Stories include: The Break, Cry Wolf, Genesis, Law of Conservation, Lightning Doesn't Strike Twice, and Paved Paradise.

Warning: This title contains graphic language and sex.

QUICKIES
By Selena Kitt

Whether the story is about a quick encounter of the erotic kind or it's just a fast and furious read, here is a pulse-pounding twenty-five story anthology, promising to take you on a headlong express to ecstasy. Join Selena Kitt on a swift, delightful ride, from stories of heart-racing sex in elevators or across office desks or in dressing rooms, to the impatience and excitement of the first time experience - you're sure to have a blissful ride on the these racing rapids of erotica!

Warnings: This title contains graphic language, explicit sex, nonconsent, prostitution, sibling incest and lesbian and m/f/f group sex.

SHIVERS
By Selena Kitt

Eight darkly erotic and horrifically delicious stories guaranteed to give you shivers, in more ways than one! Stories include: The Velvet Choker, Pumpkin Eater, The Ride, Mercy, Advent Calendar, Silent Night, The Laundry Chute and The Gingerbread Man.

Warning: This title contains graphic language, sex and erotic horror.

FALLING DOWN
By Selena Kitt

Lindsey is a bad girl, and she's determined to stay that way. She's been called a slut enough to know it's true, and she's not ashamed of the fact anymore. She makes it known to every man she comes in contact with that she's available for the taking—the rougher, the better. When she meets Lieutenant Zachary Davis, she finally finds a man who refuses to treat her like the trash she believes she really is. But can Lindsey change her wayward, dangerous ways and learn to value herself the way the Zach seems to?

Warning: This title contains graphic language and nonconsensual sex.

THE REAL MOTHER GOOSE
By Selena Kitt

Settle yourself in for a wicked bed time story, a hot, wild ride through nursery rhymes like you've never heard them before. Set in a fantastical world where the privileged few own and raise sex slaves like beloved pets, Mother herself is the star of the show, wielding a riding crop and taking care of and training her young charges with a firm and skillful hand. But where has Father Goose wandered off to, and who will take Mother in hand when she ventures too far?

Warnings: This title contains graphic language, sex, and elements of bdsm.

STARGAZING
By Selena Kitt

Turn up your collar, feather your hair, put that big comb in your back pocket, and splash on some Polo, because we're going back to high school in the '80's! Sara is obsessed with pop star Tyler Vincent, and as she nears the end of her senior year, she's determined to find a way to be with him - although her best friend, Aimee, keeps telling her to find a different escape from her desperately violent home life.

Complications arise when Dale, the mysterious new transfer student, sets his sights on Sara, and she falls for this rock-star-in-the-making in spite of her better judgment. When Sara wins a contest, she is faced with a choice - travel to Tyler Vincent's home town to meet him, or stay and support Dale in a Battle-of-the-Bands hosted by MTV. Their triangulated relationship is pushed to its breaking point, but there is another, deeper secret that Dale's been keeping that just may break things wide open...

TRUTH OR DARE
By Selena Kitt

Dare has always been the hothead in the pair – her twin, Nick, he was the calm, cool and collected one. But now Nick is dead, found murdered in their local cemetery, and Dare, on forced leave from her job as a Chicago police officer, goes back to her childhood home to attend the funeral.

It becomes quickly apparent to Dare that the local authorities aren't being straight with her, or anyone else, about what's been going on in the little Midwestern town she grew up in. The detective in her kicks in and she decides to find out what—or who—has killed her brother, so she moves in temporarily with her father and stepmother, takes a job in a local bar, and starts asking questions.

Her focus soon fixes on Shane, her brother's best friend—the town bad boy and bad seed. The tension between the two of them has always been palpable, and nothing has changed. Sparks fly as they collide, and while Dare finds herself sinking in deeper with Shane, the mystery of what happened to her brother—and an ever growing list of victims—grows even stranger.

Dare finds her past haunting her everywhere she goes as she continues to dig deeper into the circumstances of her brother's death, and her future looms large as her fate as a police officer is about to be determined back in Chicago. With everything coming to a head, she focuses on one thing: *What happened the night her brother was killed in the cemetery?* She's sure Shane knows... *something...* and she's determined to find out what it is, one way or another.

Warnings: This title contains graphic language, sex, violence and elements of horror.